STATION MASTER, EBURRU
and other stories

ALSO BY PHEROZE NOWROJEE

Pio Gama Pinto: Patriot for Social Justice

A Vote for Kenya: The Elections and the Constitution

A Kenyan Journey

Conserving the Intangible

Dukawalla and Other Stories

(with Villoo Nowrojee)
*Zanzibar Plates: Maastricht and Other Ceramics
on the East African Coast*

STATION MASTER, EBURRU

and other stories

Pheroze Nowrojee

MANQA books

NAIROBI

Published by Manqa Books
www.manqa.net

Editing by Villoo Nowrojee and Edward Miller
Book design by Edward Miller
Text set in Adobe Garamond Pro

First Edition
10 9 8 7 6 5

To
ZARIN
with love

It is the business of fiction to seem probable.

—A. S. Byatt, *On Histories and Stories*

Station Master, Eburru

THE POLICE PROSECUTOR'S voice rose higher. 'The Accused has been active in all parts of the country, fomenting disaffection and discontent. The evidence is clear. Prosecution Witness No. 1 has given evidence that the said newspaper is found regularly distributed throughout the provinces and that the Accused…'

The Magistrate, who had already made up his mind early on in the proceedings to convict this turbaned upstart in front of him, and had already sketched the outlines of the judgment in his mind, raised his head in boredom to look out of the courtroom window. Placid civil service housing returned his gaze. It did not prove a sufficient diversion on a hot Nairobi afternoon of the summer months.

Reluctantly he returned to the irritating voice aimed at him. 'The published material is before the Court. The Accused in the editorial of 4th

December 1949 published the words that have been set out in the Charge Sheet. This was sedition. This was an outrage aimed against the Empire. No respect was shown to the Royal Family. The ungrateful…'

'I doubt that Their Majesties have been unduly disturbed,' the Magistrate remarked in mild protest at the unrestrained rhetoric that the prosecutor was slipping into. The Magistrate was a demobbed solicitor who had voted for the new government at home, where imperial enthusiasm had died in the brave years of the War just concluded. Coming out from that changed society, colonial Kenya and its assumptions were a throwback to attitudes for which he had little sympathy.

The prosecutor, one of the younger sons of a Settler family near Nakuru, was however shocked by this flippancy, and thrown off balance. This really was quite improper, he thought.

'Your Honour,' he said in surprise, 'these nasty publications are widely read by Indians and Natives. They create a very bad impression against the Crown.' The Magistrate yawned discreetly and nodded. The prosecutor, thinking his protest had met with approval, carried on.

'The Accused has had a checkered career. He has had several occupations and has not retained any employment for long. He is an unreliable person. He came to the colony in 1926 as a station master on the Uganda Railway. He was sent up-country and was posted…'

The accused, Gopal Ramdass, brought up his head slowly, his eyes looking beyond the room. 1926? Was it that long ago? He could still see it in his mind so clearly.

The shrill whistle from the Guard rolled over the windy barrenness. From the middle of the cleared earth that served as the platform, Gopal Ramdass raised his right hand and waved the green flag, which had been unfurled and at the ready. The engine's whistle answered him. In a small flurry of sound and rising steam, the train slowly pulled away, and very quickly the red rear of the guard's van diminished into the distance.

No one had disembarked at the station. No one had embarked. The three men in *shukas* who had been watching the arrival and departure drifted away into the bush. This was the daily invasion of two minutes each way, a total of four minutes in every twenty-four hours with which Gopal Ramdass justified his monthly wages.

In the remaining hours, a few goods trains passed through, slowing down to drop the tablet that had allowed them to enter the section to the station, and to collect the new tablet that allowed them to move into the next section of this one-track system. Gopal Ramdass would oversee all this. He would next return to the signal box, pull the signal lever back, and wait to hear the long wires move on the small pulleys with a brief jangle. The heavy signal arm would rise back to the halt position and lock in. He would then walk slowly to his house.

Though it was the station master's house, it was only a small wood and iron structure, not a grand bungalow like those at junctions such as Nakuru, Konza, or Voi, with wooden cross-meshes along their long verandahs and many rooms. This was Eburru, only a halt, really. It followed Gilgil and preceded Elementeita on the way to the Lake. The old volcano, now covered in shrub and tall grass, rose a little behind them, but it was not a high mountain and was without the dramatic outline of nearby Longonot. For days, apart from the staff of the passing trains and his own gangers, he saw nobody. The station was completely off the rough road to Nakuru, and no Settler needed to pass the station to and from the farm. Here the wind was his only companion as it blew over the unfrequented station and the desolate emptiness around it.

The straying smoke of the engine stayed for a while above the distance and then as it too blew away, Gopal Ramdass returned to his thoughts. If only he could be free of having to work at this mechanical occupation, which did not even occupy him for more than a few minutes each day, he could apply himself to the real issue that was before everybody these days—freedom. The British were in India. They had no right to be there. Then he would always think, the British were also in Kenya. And again, they had no right to be in Kenya. They should go. They should be sent away. He would do his small share of that task here.

A newspaper was the means to expose the tyranny of these colonialists. It would reveal all the mischief that they took great pains to cover up. One day perhaps he would be a publisher, own a newspaper. He could call it the *Kenya Chronicle* or the *Colonial Mail* or something like that. The people of Kenya would read it; it would reflect their desire to be free, it would demand freedom, it would make them demand freedom. Editorials were important. Editorials of which the imperial government itself would have to take notice. London would need to ask whose pen this was that could shake them from five thousand miles away. It would confirm the savagery of this colonial oppression. It would unmask their pretence of benevolence. His editorials would show all his readers that these were not trustees, but looters and persons ready to kill.

He often set out to himself his thoughts on the issues before the country, such as the colour bar ('If those of inferior achievement demand priority by reason only of the colour of their skin…') or the right to speak freely ('The continued exile of those who speak up deters no one and is a shame condemned by all right-thinking…') or the land question ('Equality for all the subjects of the Crown is…'). Recently he had been turning over in his mind the right words for an editorial on the common roll ('If all are subjects in Kenya, then all subjects must have the same rights and obligations…' or 'No subject in Kenya can be denied the vote on the basis of…').

As these thoughts swirled around in his mind every day, his departmental returns to Nairobi would sometimes be late. Sometimes staff items would not be off-loaded. Locomotive Department memoranda began to come to him. First, they drew his attention to missing records. Then they sent reminders, and more. They even drew his attention to possible disciplinary action. After several through trains had to stop at his station because signals were not in place for the trains to pass, he received a final letter. The Kenya and Uganda Railway Administration regretted that, despite several warnings, due to the passive manner in which he attended to his duties and his lack of initiative, his services had been terminated.

The prosecutor's voice rising again in outrage brought Gopal Ramdass back to the courtroom. Pulling at the khaki shorts of his colonial uniform, his young face redder, the prosecutor wound up his earnest plea. 'This is not the first prosecution against this Accused. He has admitted that this is the fourth time he has been brought to court on the publication of anti-government matter. He was charged in 1938. He was again charged during the War. He was charged in 1948. And he is now charged again. He has been warned several times. But he has persisted in his seditious writing. There is an unfortunate readership for this across the colony. He has also admitted that he has been convicted each time, and that in 1948, only a year ago, he served a sentence of six months. If Your Honour finds him guilty, this will be his fourth conviction.'

This was indeed the case, for over the past fifteen years Gopal Ramdass had gradually emerged as a major thorn in the Governor's side and an important centre of dissent and nationalist noise. He had not only become a centre of Indian opposition in the colony, but by printing the native vernacular nationalist newspapers and notices also become a critical auxiliary to the native demands for representation which were hardening throughout the colony.

The prosecutor came to an end, 'He is a persistent offender, a terrible person, and these editorials are really bad. We really cannot allow them, sir.'

'Yes, Mr Kapila, do you want to say anything?' the Magistrate turned to the defence lawyer. He wrote down the latter's submission. 'Judgment tomorrow morning,' he mumbled as he rose and, without waiting for the bows of prosecutor and counsel, walked quickly out of the courtroom.

Two days later, the *Colonial Mail*, Gopal Ramdass's own newspaper, reported prominently, 'Editor Found Guilty. Six Months Hard Labour.' But by this time, this was no unknown minor rag from some insignificant outpost. The *Colonial Mail* was a major paper in East Africa and was known by all who had to deal with the increasing problems of Kenya. Accordingly, the national papers in Britain picked up the story too (from *The Times*: 'The recent War was not fought to muzzle…'; from the *Manchester Guardian*: 'Colony's Publisher Jailed Again… The Governor is ill-advised to keep incarcerating a person who practices the very virtues his administration preaches'). When the matter was brought up at Question Time in the House of Commons by Fenner Brockway, MP, cables had to move between the Deputy Secretary in the Colonial Office and Government House in Nairobi. The Settler daily in Kenya then had to take notice and reported the exchange in the House—reluctantly, but fully.

When Gopal Ramdass was taken to the gates of the prison to commence his sentence, a small band of supporters awaited him there. As he was taken out of the old Black Maria, they cheered. The priest of the Arya Samaj came forward. Prayers were said for his safety. An indulgent prisons officer did not disturb the many speeches praising Gopal Ramdass before he was led in.

The next morning, at the Rift Valley Sports Club, Nakuru, with an *East African Standard* open before him at the page reporting Gopal Ramdass's imprisonment, one of the readers said,

'I used to know this chap. I think I wrote the letter sacking him from the Railways.'

'Should have left him there,' said another. 'By all accounts it would have been a bloody lot less trouble for everybody.'

Learning

THE TWO BOYS were walking back from the games field. They were carrying on an earlier argument of the day. Rupert said earnestly, 'My father was at the farewell to the Governor.' Rupert's father had worked in the Treasury during a past Governor's term, and had been regularly at Government House. 'My father says that Grigg then said that "all of us who represent the British race must keep up the standard of our civilization and see that our children maintain them too". That is us. We are those children. Grigg should know. We must follow what he says. Do you know he is now *Lord* Altrincham? He sits in the House of Lords!'

His close friend replied gently. 'It's very serious. Do you know we number no more than ten thousand in the whole country, yet there are already a thousand boys in our school? Very few of our parents can afford to send us to a school like this in England. But there are many more than only one thousand boys in Kenya who qualify to attend this school, and we must spend such money on all the boys in Kenya whatever their race is, fairly.'

'But John, we, we must have the best schools. We need them.' He had the bright alert look of the young who have been raised as superior. In the presence of the subordinated populace, and conscious always of its watchful eye on them, the adults acted out a role rather than lived. The role held out that they were naturally equipped with a solution for every problem afflicting the ruled and themselves. And their young emulated the stance. Rupert continued eagerly, 'Only the other day, Lord Francis Scott said in the Legislative Council: "There can be no dispute that in a country of mixed races, such as Kenya, where European children are eventually going to be in a position of authority over other races, especially the natives, it is essential they should be as well educated as is possible."'

'Things are changing, Rupert. The world is changing. This is 1941. This War is changing the world. And our colony will also be changed.'

'But surely we will still have to give the orders. How else will the farms do well? Who else will tell the juniors in government what to do?'

'It may not be so always. Things will not be the same after the war. We do not need all this only for ourselves,' and John waved his hand over the expansive school grounds and the many imposing buildings.

The school had been designed by the foremost colonial British architect, Sir Herbert Baker. Baker had been the assistant to Sir Edward Luytens, who had planned and designed the imperial capital of New Delhi in India. Thereafter, Baker had been sent to the African Settler colonies. There he had designed the imposing government buildings of South Africa's capital, Pretoria, and then come to Kenya where he had designed the new Government House (much later to be called State House), the Law Courts, the Railway Headquarters, and the main schools for the Settler children.

Baker's task for these latter was to set their schooling within a frame that would reflect the responsible privilege and pomp that would attend their future. The students in these newly designed schools were being programmed to rule: to wear the unquestionable belief in the superiority of one race, their own, over the self-evident inferiority of others; to henceforth act on those assumptions; to know that those assumptions would be unwaveringly upheld in their favour by the colony's authorities, even when they were manifestly wrong; to assume that this unnatural belief was normal and right; to assume at improper ages the decision-making powers over swathes of older persons.

Part of the confidence to do so was their unquestioned childhood right to habitation of buildings and facilities such as these that would deliberately be denied to those over whom they would rule. It was to be, and was, a denial to those other children of the tools of dignity and government. The buildings stood as a clear statement of the place and the future of those other children in the scheme of things in the colony's future. The denial of their admittance to those buildings followed.

John's hand as it moved encompassed the school's golf course and swimming pool, which they were passing. He continued, 'We do not need this for only a few Kenyans and not others. All boys should…'

'But John,' his friend interrupted him quickly, 'Sir Edward Grigg himself said that if we did not give the best education to our people, "we could soon be saddled with a rapidly increasing burden of uneducated 'poor whites'". Do you want that?'

'Rupert, you are clever. You will go on to university in England next year. And one or two of us too. But the others in our class won't. And there are also *other* clever boys in Kenya who could go to university if they were in our school. But they are not allowed to join our school. Nor do their own schools get the good things we have in our school, things which would help them get to university, which now they do not attend.'

'But you do think this is a good school, don't you?'

'Of course.'

'You wouldn't want its good things taken away?'

'No,' replied John, 'But they should not be

only for a few. It would be…,' he fumbled for the word, '…right, if they were for all the colony. For all qualified boys in the colony. And for all to be able to attend this school.'

The dinner bell rang. And the exchange came to an end. For the time being. Arms around each other's shoulders, the two friends went into the hall.

Just Like Us

'BUT YOU ENGLISH always keep your word,' said Mr Pandit. There was a silence. 'What happened?'

Mr Pandit was talking to Mr Wise, who owned the fancy clothing shop across the road. Mr Wise had come to Gilgil only a few years ago. Their common interest as traders had made them acquaintances first, and then a little more. On occasion they might even be seen in each other's shop, passing a few moments on the way to or from other business.

By the time Mr Wise had come to Gilgil, Mr Pandit's family had been there many decades, and their shop, Eburru Provision Stores, had become an institution for the Settlers around, from Eburru and Elementeita to Ol Kalou and Thomson's Falls. Shopping there was the foundation for months on the farm, before another foray was necessary. Mr Pandit's shelves held necessities, but also delicacies, and when the end of the year approached, seasonal luxuries also appeared on the counter. Christmas pudding jars with cloth caps stood invitingly next to open boxes of Christmas crackers. Strings of dark green paper chains, simulating bunches of holly, would hang from parts of the ceiling. Cotton wool reminded the customers of the snow they had fled from, which they yet recalled here at the Equator with much insincere nostalgia.

When times were good, the Settlers were good customers. Then Mr Pandit's family was kept busy, and Mr Pandit did well. When times were hard and money was tight, Mr Pandit was a good shopkeeper and extended long credit to his regulars. And both sides honoured that understanding, one which was never written down between them. It came with Mr Pandit from the commerce of the East, and with the Settlers from the honour of their word, and here in the Rift Valley both found receptive Kenyan soil.

Right now, in the continuing Depression of the mid-1930s, times were hard. Both Mr Pandit and Mr Wise had more time to spend talking than serving behind the counter. And so it was that the empty shop had been the setting for Mr Wise's confidence and Mr Pandit's remark, 'But you English always keep your word.'

In the silence, Mr Wise remembered the journey from Europe. But it was not from England, not from Tilbury. Along with many, most unknown to each other, and from different places, carrying a half-empty cardboard suitcase, his journey had begun on a chartered tramp. It had moved out of Trieste to an unknown future eastward. There was no booking that he had made, and he had had no right to ask destinations. Other caring and determined minds had fashioned not travel, but escape, and the ship had moved slowly, down into the Mediterranean and then to Egypt. They had been unprepared for the heat, which had increased in the basin of the Suez Canal. At Aden, the ship had stopped for a day. Then, for several days. Someone somewhere was deciding where to send them, first asking who would receive them.

The decision, when it came, sent Mr Wise's boat down towards the Equator; they were going to South Africa. When the ship reached Mombasa, it lay at anchor for a few days. Eventually, a few of the passengers were allowed to disembark. Mr Wise was among them and he enjoyed the prospect of being on land again. They went into town, and Mr Wise saw the thriving shops on Salim Road and on Kilindini Avenue, and he felt he could do business in Mombasa as well as in any place in South Africa, though of course the choice was not his. They were returning to the ship when they heard a greeting in a language they had not been addressed in for the past many weeks.

An animated conversation had followed, many questions from the elderly man who had spoken to them, a few answers from the group. But the man had turned out to be from Mr Wise's home-place in Europe. The outcome was that the next morning the man took Mr Wise to the Mombasa Immigration Office.

'What is your name?'

'Josif Weisz.'

The official handed over a temporary visa. It allowed Joseph Wise to stay in the country for three months. And eventually, Mr Wise had been granted permanent residence and reached Gilgil.

Now Mr Wise thought, *Did I keep my word?* He certainly had never intended otherwise. He came from a business family, and he was keenly aware that his family would consider that when he had given his word on a transaction, his honour, their honour, was at stake, regardless of what any document said.

After he had been in the country a few weeks, it had been arranged that he would be settled in Gilgil, and a bank had been spoken to there to advance a loan to enable him to set up shop. This was all he had dreamed of since he had left Europe, and though Mr Jennings, the manager in the small branch there, had been a bit rough, and though the formalities had been stretched out by Mr Jennings more than perhaps they should have been, Mr Wise had been grateful. For the first year he had had no difficulty in meeting the repayments. But as the Depression bit into the farming community who were his customers, he began to get late with his repayments, and then to default for longer periods. He had taken every step he could to effect economies and sought to collect in every amount he was owed. But every time he had brought in something, the interest accruing at the month's end had raised the debt level even higher.

Mr Jennings had therefore loomed large in this past year. Constant demands from Mr Jennings and constant visits to Mr Jennings: this humiliating daily fare had gnawed at Mr Wise's equanimity. Now, the blow that Mr Jennings had threatened him with for so many months had finally fallen. He had received the letter from Mr Jennings demanding total repayment of the outstanding debt within two weeks and serving notice that, failing that, the business would be sold off. Mr Wise could see no way out, least of all by repayment of the total outstanding due.

It was in such a moment of helplessness and resignation that he had let slip the matter to Mr Pandit, and Mr Pandit had then remarked, 'But you English always keep your word.'

Mr Pandit saw an immediate solution. 'Go and see Mr Jennings. He is like you, he will help you.'

'No, he will not help.'

'Of course he will. You English people always help each other.'

There was a pause.

'No.' He saw Mr Pandit's puzzled face. 'I have never been to England. They will not help me. They are not even letting me join their Club.'

Mr Pandit was shocked. There was a long, long silence. At last Mr Pandit said, 'But then… you are just like us.'

Mr Pandit was deeply upset by Mr Wise's impending collapse. It preyed on him, and in his mind he began to seek ways out for Mr Wise. It was in one of these uncharacteristic moods that his good customer, the District Medical Officer, Dr Macdonald, found him a few days later.

'Pandit, you look distinctly down in the mouth. What's the matter?'

'Nothing, nothing.'

'I trust Mrs Pandit is well? Let me have some of my usual, will you? Are the children alright?'

'Oh, yes.' Mr Pandit placed the two bottles of whisky on the counter. But as he went about getting the other items on the doctor's list, the doctor thought he could never remember Pandit so gloomy, and he determined to extract the cause.

'Are you unwell?'

'Not me, Doctor.'

'Then who?'

'Someone.' But encouraged by the doctor's sympathetic tone, Mr Pandit hesitantly added, 'It is Mr Wise.'

'Is he sick?'

'No, no. I cannot help him. He is in difficulty.'

The doctor waited.

'The bank is selling his shop next week.'

The doctor thought for a moment, then said sharply, 'Not that man Jennings again?'

Mr Jennings, as the bank manager, was by custom the Treasurer at the Club. Like the other clubs that colonial officialdom established all over the Empire, Gilgil Club was the bastion of safety against insurrection and the native multitude. But it was also the social arbiter within the white community. Its exclusiveness taught the natives their place in the racial hierarchy, but also the members of the Club theirs in the white hierarchy.

Mr Wise's application, duly proposed and duly seconded, had reached the Club Committee some months ago. Even before the Balloting Committee could look at it, Jennings had made it the subject of discussion in the Managing Committee. He had been vocal against the admission of people of this kind. They would all remember what had happened in 1904, and that was not so long ago. These people had been kept out. Good work had been done by Grogan and his friends. He was referring to the orchestrated Settler campaign of that early time to prevent the visiting Zionist Committee taking up the offer of the British Government of land in Kenya to establish their Homeland. And good work, Jennings had continued, by some wild game. There would be sniggering from Jennings and others at this point, because of the reference to the widespread propagation of an exaggerated danger of wildlife in the promised area. There was no need, Jennings would conclude, to change what was a long-established practice at the Club. And not only in this club, but in clubs all over the colony.

The discussion had split the committee and continued over into the management meetings of successive months. Jennings had leaked some of the proceedings at the Gents' Bar, and there had been some unseemly (and well-orchestrated) scenes there as well.

To Dr Macdonald, the news from Pandit seemed to be a continuation of that campaign. To him it smacked of unfairness. This was bullying in the service of an unbecoming prejudice. There was lack of professionalism in this use of the bank's powers. Jennings was pushing Wise into a situation where the refusal of his membership application could then be publicly clothed in terms of lack of financial standing, while, privately, bigotry would claim a boastful victory.

The doctor turned to Mr Pandit with a scowl. Mr Pandit resumed hesitantly, 'Yes... Mr Jennings has written the letter... Mr Jennings is a good person...but he does not like Mr Wise.'

The doctor obviously did not share Mr Pandit's view of Mr Jennings. 'I'll be back,' he barked, and walked abruptly out of the shop. He turned right, and Mr Pandit saw him headed towards the District Commissioner's Office.

It was a few days later that Mr Wise walked into Mr Pandit's shop waving a letter. He was smiling broadly, and talking too fast. 'He has listened to me, he has listened to me at last. God bless Mr Jennings. Mr Jennings has given me more time, more time, see here, see here… God bless him.'

Higher Education

WHEN HARISH BHATT was assigned to the chambers of Mr Justice Troughton, the Judge thought Harish a serious and industrious young man. He would find him poring over books in every spare moment. Harish would read them even in court when the proceedings were dull and there was no immediate need of his duties as Court Clerk, yet few were the moments when the Judge had had to rap on the bench to gain Harish's attention. That certainly was an improvement on some of the clerks, who not infrequently were inattentive because they had fallen asleep. If Harish was not paying attention in court, sensitive to the needs of either Judge or counsel in the matter of passing exhibits or authorities cited, it was only because he was deep in some volume, which he was underlining and marking conspicuously.

After a fortnight of this, Judge Troughton was sufficiently curious to commend the young man on his industry and to inquire exactly what it was that he was doing. 'Studying, my lord.' Troughton had smiled and said, 'So hard?' 'Yes, sir, I am only a matric, and I must study more.' This had seemed quite admirable to Troughton. He had asked him what it was that he was studying. 'Bookkeeping and accounts, My Lord.' Troughton had nodded sympathetically.

After a while, he had found him equally dedicated to another set of thin books. 'No, sir,' Harish had answered in response to the query, 'I finished Accounts. I am waiting for my results. I sat the exam last week. It will go to London,' he continued, in awe of his own achievement in having his paper marked by a person who was so important he worked in London. 'So what are you reading now?' 'I am doing Elementary French now, My Lord.'

When the Bookkeeping Certificate came in, it was a proud Harish who brought it to show to the Judge. The Judge commended him and had been pleased to do so, for Harish's achievements were not at the expense of the satisfactory performance of his duties. At the end of the term, the

Elementary French Certificate from the French Consulate had followed, though Troughton had smiled at the thought of Harish in a Parisian café on the Left Bank.

They had then broken for the summer vacation of the law courts. It was not summer in Kenya. Actually, it was winter, for this vacation commenced on the first day of August of each year, and the months of June, July, and August constituted Kenya's cold season. But it was summer in Britain. So the vacation in those winter months of the Kenya Colony nevertheless became the summer vacation of its courts. This legal fiction made the title congruent with the hope in the minds of the Judges that, as it was now summer where they came from, they might with a lot of luck have their leave applications approved, so as to be able to spend them at 'home' when there was some bearable weather. It was one of the perks of owning a colony, that by subsidiary legislation, the Chief Justice could turn winter into summer, and deem the current weather of Britain to be the current weather of Kenya, a useful, if doubtful, legal proposition.

When they resumed after the vacation, Harish was seen busy scribbling. The Judge had noted this and after a while had quietly looked at some discarded efforts. He found that Harish was learning Pitman's shorthand. He often saw stuffed brown paper envelopes addressed to Harish at the law courts post office box number from the British Tutorial College in London.

That term was a busy one for Harish, but soon he was showing another certificate to the Judge. By the following Easter he must also have begun the overlooked Typing Part I, because the Judge saw Miss Pinto, his secretary, sometimes allow Harish a brief practice session and a demonstration from her. The increasing certificates were prominently, if with studied carelessness, left on his table for all to see.

It was in the Typing I class that Harish met Miss Sharadha Joshi, a fellow pupil. Harish was smitten. It was not long before he had informed Miss Pinto of the event. Miss Pinto, with a clearer eye to our social structures, deftly, but in kindly fashion, soon elicited the fact that Harish had never talked to the young lady, that Miss Joshi was unaware of his existence, and that Miss Joshi's parents were of particularly orthodox persuasion. To move his undeclared suit forward, Harish discussed the best ways with the sympathetic Miss Pinto, an incurable romantic whose drawer could always be counted upon to be holding the latest *True Love* or *Silver Screen*. She made practical suggestions. 'Go up to her and tell her how good her remarks in class were.' 'But she never speaks in class,' he would moan. 'Help her with her books.' 'Her brother always comes to do that.' At last Harish figured it out. He would impress Miss Joshi. So, he told Miss Pinto, he had enrolled in front of Miss Joshi for two classes that term. 'She saw me giving my forms to the teacher, and I think she smiled.' Miss Pinto did not think that constituted much of an introduction strategy, but said nothing. At her Railway Goan Institute dances, that was never a problem.

Harish was soon visible in the lunch hour busy on the small lawn below the Chief Justice's window, and as the weeks passed circles began to appear under his eyes. The two courses were beginning to tell. But he came back one morning full of smiles, and after court had adjourned he was immediately with Miss Pinto giving her the news. Miss Joshi had at last spoken to him.

The tutor had announced that Harish had stood at the top of the class in both the subjects. When all the students had come to collect their certificates, her father had been with Miss Joshi. She had been very admiring of his achievement and had praised him. She had introduced Harish to her father and told him Harish was working in the law courts. When his certificates had been given to him by the college clerk, she had said to her father, 'He is very clever.' Harish had felt he had scaled Mount Everest while simultaneously holding aloft Mount Gowardhan like Lord Krishna. He felt the thought was a good omen, for Lord Krishna looked favourably upon young lovers.

As if in confirmation, he learned that she had enrolled for the Typing Intermediate course. Immediately Harish had enrolled for the Intermediate course and for another two: Surveying and one of the LCC Exams. This was to impress her and, more importantly, to impress her parents. This aspect was becoming more critical, because he had been able to meet her mother once. The old lady had simpered over him, since, though he did not know it, and would not gather its significance even if it were handed to him on a silver *thali*, she still had three unmarried daughters to go, Sharadha would already be twenty next year, and she had checked that he was of the right, and highest, caste.

Now he was studying furiously in court, and out of it. A new fear came over him: the possibility of failing. He became convinced that if he failed any of the papers it would destroy the relationship. He would not be considered fit for her. Her parents would never allow the suit. He would be lowered in their eyes forever. He began to work harder.

So when she suggested they meet in the evenings, he made excuses, for he had to complete his readings for each day. Her mother invited him to come on the weekends, but that was when he would study the most, and he shyly declined. The same happened in respect of public holidays. He found himself torn between the two calls. Yet he was determined that he must study hard and finish these three courses at one go, and then, and only then, would he be considered worthy to send someone to ask for her hand in marriage.

Then, he became aware of something that was inexplicable to him. The harder he studied, the less approving the desirable Miss Joshi appeared to become. After a while of deep doubt, he confided in Miss Pinto. 'She is not seeming happy with me.' Miss Pinto asked the appropriate questions and ascertained that she was not smiling as much, or even much. That when he said goodbye after each class and rushed off to study, she was getting curt in her farewells. That in an effort to change this, he had once suggested that they have some tea in the café downstairs after the class, 'Just quickly, for a few minutes.' She had said she was busy. But then he had found her at the corner of the street, lounging about in leisurely fashion with the girls in the class. Did Miss Pinto think that if he enrolled for two more courses Miss Joshi would look upon him as kindly as before? He told Miss Pinto that he was studying like that so that he could offer her his hand as someone who was a qualified and responsible person.

'I am already studying as hard as I can,' he said haltingly. 'There is no time to study any more, but I could try.' Miss Pinto dissuaded him, and tried to explain that it might be that he needed to do the opposite. But he was hardly listening any more, and he would not have believed it had he been listening. When the end of that year came and he brought his new, and largest, crop of certificates to show her, but despondently, Miss Pinto's worst fears were realized. He had stood at the top of the class again, but Miss Joshi had announced that morning to the class that she was leaving the next day for Mombasa to marry the priest's son there. She had brought the traditional box of sweets for the class to celebrate her engagement to the young man, who she had not yet seen.

When Miss Pinto confidentially explained to Mr Justice Troughton why his clerk was no longer the man he used to be, Judge Troughton thought of his own achievement in obtaining the Letters

Patent appointing him a Puisne Judge, and won-
dered whether in gaining the one, he might have
lost more of his own wife than he realized.

Initiation

'HOW BUT IN CUSTOM and in ceremony are innocence and beauty born?' asked W. B. Yeats in a prayer for his daughter. But when you are in a country far away from where those customs and those ceremonies are, innocence and beauty have other begetters too, and must also find other wet nurses. The transport of ourselves to Kenya by dhows or tiny ill-crowded steamers on large oceans was itself an unsure exercise. The carriage of additional baggage, such as custom and ceremony, was an even less certain enterprise. We were carrying only what a colonial authority would allow, and those customs and ceremonies might well have been frowned on. There was leakage too during the passage, so that over ocean and time, some custom and ceremony was lost overboard. Some was replaced, till we were perhaps innocent and beautiful, but only by reason of other customs, or partly of our customs and partly of those of others. And beauty too was other features, or a mix of features.

We were Parsees, far away from western India and the daily rituals of our fire temples. Here in Nairobi, we had no annual rhythms of ceremonies and attendance in them, which would imprint upon us and then carry us forward for the rest of our lives. The mass celebrations of the birth of our prophet, or his death, or the entry of the equinox or the birth of a ruler were major celebrations in India, not here. By such rhythms, year after year children grow, imbibe the past, look back on a childhood of regular beat and steady growth, not one of irregular spikes of highs and lows.

There were funerals here of course, there were prayers of course. But while we were its devotees, we had never seen a fire temple. There was none in our city, none in our country. There were weddings. There, for us, were crowds. But much later when we saw the records, we could see that when the whole Parsee community of the city had assembled, there were no more than a hundred and twenty persons present at its largest moments. So we grew up with seldom more than a hundred persons who shared with us, simultaneously, race, religion, residence, and language. A hundred was a large number for a child. But later, we realized its translation into a 'crowd' was meaningless, and thus we had no reliable benchmark in formulating a perception of the world as we grew up. And so my view of the world became, and has remained, that of so few like me and very many of others, different, who are interesting to look at and to find more about. It made me look outwards, and therefore in the years ahead brought a greater understanding of the larger environment around me. It gave me an inexhaustible opportunity to learn of the new.

Our infrequent Parsee ceremonies gave me no understanding of ritual, but only a pleasurable sense of uniqueness, as hardly any school friends shared them with me. We were away from the principal celebrants, head priests and scholars, and far away from the places of pilgrimage and homage, which were on a different continent.

Here we claimed to be Parsees, but we were really only camp followers, sidelined by distance and left behind by the passage of years. We were in a time machine that had impelled us neither forward nor backward, but merely laterally to a standstill.

In Kenya, we claimed to have a cultural rhythm, but really we were a mixture of rhythms, with some of ours, and much of many others. That again meant that some of ours had given way. The adult world's competing claims of profit and purity also took their toll on us children. The authorities decreed that we break our schools for four weeks to celebrate the one day of Christmas, and break for one day for Diwali, which we celebrated for four weeks in our neighbourhood. It is astonishing how easily children accept the most illogical of adult behaviour. The Indian shops publicly displayed ersatz components of festivity learned secondhand: cotton wool snow, Christmas crackers, card fir tree. Yet often when Idd and Diwali and Navroz came, we were in the middle of exams, the colony keeping to its rhythms and not ours. But to us children, all this seemed completely natural.

This was no rhythm, or if it were, it was in split

time, and we grew up with split custom and split ceremonies, and earned perhaps split innocence and split beauty. There were advantages. We enjoyed ourselves hugely, celebrating not only our festivals and holidays, but everybody else's too. It made us adaptable, it prepared us for the shifts we would have to make thirty and forty years later over continents and places. It made us adept at leading double lives. So later when we were components of an exodus and had tags marked expellee on our lapels, when—neglected by both media and history—we were forced to move, we were equipped better than we thought. We had become able to be this *and* that, to live here and there, and, despite all that, still to hold on to those strange ceremonies we never fully learned.

So we came to our rites of passage in a mix that neither our spiritual rulers far away nor our temporal rulers in this small colony, nor our local priest, nor our parents, nor Yeats, nor our nine-year-old selves could wholly unravel. And in this unresolvable melee, the big day was announced. My cousin and I would have our Navjote on our New Year's Day in two months' time. It was the ceremony of confirmation into our ancient Zoroastrian faith.

We had been learning our prayers for a long time and reciting them by rote in Avestan Pahlavi, the old language of our scriptures. We had to do this to the satisfaction of the priest and our grandmother and our mothers. But now the occasion was imminent.

As the Navjote approached, our minds were filled with the expectation of presents, serious presents like fountain pens or wrist watches, which then were the acme of gifts and the acknowledgment of adulthood. But the latter was accomplished most of all by the announcement that we were to be fitted out in suits. This meant a jacket, matching shorts, and a tie. That was not really a suit. It was many years before we finally obtained long trousers—or matching long trousers at that. But for now we were content. The shorts were to match the jacket and both were to be woollen. That, in our limited lexicon, was a 'suit', anything woollen was a 'suit'.

Our indulgent Prophet, Zarathustra, who

seldom prescribed any harsh penance for his followers and extolled the virtues of good living, was, I am sure, forgiving of us when, as the day neared, we two boys viewed the event as one where we were to acquire our First Suit, rather than our Good Religion.

Into this qualified rite of half a passage into half a suit, another big day arrived. My cousin and I were to be taken to Dharmal Bharmal & Co., Tailors and Outfitters to be measured.

There we entered a deep and vast hall, apprehensive and ready, like all pilgrims, to be awed. High pillars and recesses on each side strengthened the feeling that we had entered sacred enclosures. The people in it spoke in hushed tones. To us, who had so far been users only of lowly cottons, the smell of clean, quality wool humbled us. But when we caught sight of a solitary figure standing amidst those bales, we were terror struck. We recognized him. This was Mr Thakore. This was the man who held the power each weekend of failure or success over our heroes.

Mr Thakore was a cricket umpire. Not just someone who was casually called onto the field from among the spectators and good naturedly gave no one 'Out!' except the most obvious cases. Mr Thakore was a qualified umpire, in fact an international umpire of standing. He did not run onto the field as some organizer's afterthought. He did not make small talk at the end of overs. When loud, vociferous appeals were made, he did not say, 'What happened?' as some of our weekend umpiring stalwarts were wont to do.

Mr Thakore appeared each Sunday—for he was too important to umpire in Saturday games— in a long white coat which contrasted strikingly with his very dark visage. He wore a neat white Panama in the bright sun. He always stood leaning forward, his face inscrutable, one sharp eye on the crease for a no ball and the other on the pitch. His independent and inexorable scrutiny caused tremors in our young hearts, which were full of unwavering allegiance to our heroes, who we would never acknowledge were 'Out'. Yet we knew in our guilty hearts that the omniscient Mr Thakore had heard the click against the bat, or seen the flight going straight to the stumps while our hero had obligingly placed his big flat feet in the way. Mr Thakore missed nothing.

Now here he was standing in the shop as he stood at the crease, leaning forward at attention, his hands behind him, the stern and unmoving judge of all the action before him. He shook hands with our parents and replaced his hands behind his back, and looked down at us. He was seeing all our faults; we were sure that by now he had already seen that we did not yet know all our prayers, that those garbled words we parroted were not Avestan words, that we were in fact unworthy of a woollen suit, and one more misstep here and he would give us 'Out'.

We drew back nervously, avoiding his eye. But Mr Thakore had set a tight field. Silent and intimidating, his salesmen were placed at point, silly mid-off, silly mid-on, and, cunningly, at leg slip. As we hesitated and turned, counters rose behind us, higher than us, braces of wickets we would never be able to defend. Stacked against the tall ceiling, rows of bolts of different weaves stood behind Mr Thakore and us, huge screens on either end of the field.

Even though we had not run, indeed not even moved, Mr Thakore made a hand signal. We froze. Play had commenced. Immediately the opening bowler came at us from the boundary of our vision. The man's appearance sent ice down our veins. Blood-shot eyes and an emaciated face with uneven stubble and protruding yellow teeth bent over us. He wore a shiny vestal cord around his neck. Closer, its markings were recognizable as those of a measuring tape. It was significantly longer than either of us two. He was one of Mr Thakore's backroom tailors, let out into the light for this task.

We were first measured in concentric circles descending from our necks. Stained purple and yellow on a sallow dry skin the colour of dust, his mouth was full simultaneously of pins, an expired cigarette, and a copying pencil stub. His hands held arcs of garment chalks, several parts of the tape, and small bits of cloth specimens as he kept circling around us. This terrifying figure also played for Ngara's St. Francis Xavier Tailors Eleven, with regular and frequent encouragement from a few supporters and many glasses of *feni*, the high-octane home brew made from cashews, usually issued to those on the battlements before final kamikaze efforts.

Through his barricaded mouth, sullen mumbles came forth. Another of Mr Thakore's team transmuted these strange sounds into a large leather-bound ledger in a cuneiform not as yet the subject of any archaeological discovery. We looked at what he had marked, but nothing in our very limited education could identify its genus.

Then we were turned about many times. None of our strokes seemed to work. By now we knew we would never score. This was one more of those occasions when there would not be even polite applause when we returned to the pavilion. This would be another in the long line of that hated word, duck. We were now being measured vertically, along our backs, under our armpits, down to our knees. What little resistance we might have had was surrendered.

'Over?' Mr Thakore asked the man. But we knew it was not a question. It was only a proper statement of his Sunday duties. And a maiden one at that.

We knocked into each other in our hurry to cross over to the opposite side of the pitch, for our grounds mostly possessed only one batting end. We tried simultaneously to leave this field. No one we knew had ever thrown in a bat, or even a towel, in any match we had seen, but we were ready to do both. We could not continue. We would do whatever it took to retire, together. Holding on to each other, we tumbled out of the shop into the sunlight, and there expressed the easing of our fears and our relief in a noisy return home.

In due course our Navjote took place, and we were initiated, as yet without conviction, not into the beautiful religion we would have to rediscover for ourselves much adulthood later, but into that world of suits we had felt the need for with much greater immediacy.

Donation

THE COMMITTEE'S DELIBERATIONS fell silent, unresolved. The issue had been discussed again and again, and no solution had emerged. The problem was the financing of the last unit in the small social service complex in the community's yard. For the kitchen and the modest meeting place, they had raised the funds steadily from within the community. Now, members did not seem keen to part with the required balance. The War had just ended, and Nairobi in February 1946 could not yet be considered a booming economy.

'We shall have to go back to Sethia.' This was the most prominent individual in the small community, not otherwise noted for its wealth. The title Sethia was an acknowledgement that his prominence extended beyond the small community to the broader trading brotherhood. For Sethia was the highest title in the peerage of the colony's Gujarati commerce. It was he who had been the largest of the previous donors. It was he who had many years ago put up the community's own temple. He had come to Nairobi before the First World War as a fourteen-year-old from a pauper rural family in arid Cutch. He had left behind parents, siblings, and his short acquaintance with education under the *pipal* tree. Then jumped on a canoe going to a midstream dhow going to he did not know where, but he knew it was going out into the ocean and some future other than this. When he climbed on that vessel, no one, not even the *nakhoda*, called him a stowaway. Instead he had found caring and giving on the long voyage.

He never forgot what he had learned almost every moment on the dhow, from those who shared what they cooked with him, or who gave him something to wear, and from the numerous conversations which went on around him. All of this had stood him in good stead upon landing in Mombasa, where one of the older passengers took him to a *duka* whose owner also was from the village he had left. It was agreed he would begin work there.

For the next two years he worked from every dawn till every dusk, without any pay. At the end of it, the time came to speak of a wage. And when the employer suggested a figure that could neither allow savings that would enable him to go back and open a shop in their village in India, nor provide enough to marry in Mombasa, he had to refuse the offer. He became despondent. But the shrewd, and kind, employer made a further offer. It emerged out of something the young man had never heard of.

It was the shared *bhaichhoro* (brotherhood) within the community. It was the strong duty to help each other in business, within an environment where there was no help from the government or elsewhere. And there never was any help for the *dukawalla* from the colonial government. His employer then said to him, 'I cannot pay you more than I have offered. But if you are not going back, I can help you with some goods and a small loan to open your own shop.' The young Harji had gladly accepted this new offer. A further adventure had begun. It became the foundation in time of more, much more.

After the end of the first War he had gone,

in 1919, into partnership in cotton with a friend in Uganda. At first they bought small amounts, and then, increasingly, larger amounts. Soon they were exporting to buyers on the Bombay Stock Market, and then even to Japan. He brought to these business decisions that same independent mind that, young as he had been, had made the decision to leave his birthplace. When he had left, those many years ago, he had left behind somebody else's idea of his future. And made the decision that he would find his future himself. He felt an irrational certainty that it lay elsewhere, though he did not then know where. He had then placed all on his own instinct, the pull of adventure, and the firm basis that looking back was not for him. And these years had justified that trust in himself.

A ginning factory followed and another in another district. And then in others. In Kenya, the partners bought out a failing sisal plantation, and opened upmarket provision stores in Nairobi, Nakuru, and Eldoret for imported goods serving the white Settlers. Now he was a major business house, an industrialist, a nominated member of the Nairobi Municipal Council, often at Government House and in the newspapers, the latter for philanthropy in the form of classrooms and clinics. All this time he never closed the first *duka* he had opened. The partners would frequently conduct their private meetings there.

*

The Committee stood in the Sethia's presence, and shook his hand respectfully. He held out a limp hand. 'Sethia, we are sorry to bother you again.' He could not remember the Chairman, though he remembered that it was the same man who had come five years ago, some nonentity from the community.

The Chairman, who was a senior accountant in one of the government departments, cleared his throat. Then commenced in Gujarati. Consulting around before attempting this formidable task, he had been advised by his counterpart in the Medical Services to use the vernacular, as it was known in such circles that Harjibhai's hold on the English language was tenuous, and a long conversation in it would lead to public lapses on his part. This would bring about an immediate refusal. He was known to have his longer speeches in the Municipal Council dictated by him in Gujarati to his secretary and translated and typed out for him in English. This was then transcribed into Gujarati script, from which he would sound out the speech in English in the Council Chamber.

When everyone was seated, Seth Harjibhai spoke. 'You didn't do all that you promised to do with the money we have already given you.'

'Sorry, Sethia, we were not able to collect the matching money. Others are not as generous as you.' Everyone shook their heads vigorously at this self-evident truth. 'And this is the last building. We could only turn to you, the most generous member of our community and a national figure. We would be overwhelmed…and the community would be forever grateful. We would of course write to you acknowledging,' and ascending into English, the Chairman concluded, 'another most munificent gift.' Other members of the committee continued earnestly for another quarter of an hour, that it would be an asset to all, and how much the new building was necessary in order to obtain the certificate of occupation for the whole project. They all emphasized that it was the only part left to complete.

'Very well, we'll think about it. We'll write.'

Quite soon the letter came. It said, 'We are pleased to give this donation on condition that the building comes up quickly and that it be named on the outside prominently after my late and honoured wife, Bai Putlibai Harjibai.'

The committee members were shattered. The meeting that was immediately called was mostly silent. It seemed there was no way forward. Finally they agreed on a request for a further audience with the Sethia. Urgent messages were sent to him.

He received them graciously, even though he was not exactly pleased with their unenthusiastic response to the terms of the letter. After tea had been served and there had been enough bowing and scraping, he said, 'Well, we have thought about it and will give you the donation, and it will be named after my late wife.'

The Chairman's face fell in response. The Sethia saw that. His displeasure returned. He spoke louder. 'This is what you wanted. Now when I have given it to you, you refuse to name it after my wife. Why are you against this? And if you are not, how dare you refuse a proper request in her honour? This is ingratitude. You wouldn't want me to become angry.'

'No, no, no,' several voices spoke up at once. 'We would never want you to be angry with us. With all your generosity to us all, we would never intend such a thing to happen.'

'Well then, go away, think about what I have said, and come back when you are ready, with the drawings showing how Bai Putlibai's name is over the front door of the building so all can see it. I would be pleased to open it.'

The Committee tumbled out of his large office in total disarray. And in a complete quandary. There was no one who could tell the Sethia why they had not immediately fallen into agreement with his proposal and why their hesitation had been so evident.

Months passed in this impasse. One day they got a summons from the Sethia asking if they wanted the moneys or not. They were received again.

'Well, have you reconsidered the matter of putting up my wife's name?'

'Sir,' the Chairman lapsed into the formal English opening, just as he would when speaking to his superior in the office. And, quickly returning to the preferred Gujarati, said, 'We cannot put her name on the building.'

A shadow passed over the Sethia's face. Then resignedly he said, 'I cannot force you. Well then, when do you expect the building to start construction? When do you think it would be ready for me to open it?'

'Oh, oh, oh, sir,' the Chairman, Secretary, and Treasurer spoke out in unison. 'We can never let you open it,' they said very respectfully. 'It would be wrong of us.'

'I don't like the attitude of your committee.' The Sethia's voice got louder. 'There are many buildings named after my wife, and there has never been any objection. I have opened many, many buildings. And there has been no objection to that either. You are the first ones to refuse.'

The committee members looked down.

His anger rising, the Sethia said, 'I think it is best I take back this donation.' He continued harshly, 'Since you are all so disrespectful to my wife. And so unreasonable. Yes, I think it best. What can one expect from such a committee? I think I will tell my accountant not to send anything.' And he picked up the phone on his table.

This brought the officials to their feet, crying out, 'No, no, no!' The elderly Chairman began a stuttered, 'It is the last building, sir, and...' Then his involuntary hesitation dried into a long and lonely pause.

Into this lengthening silence, Mr Kalyan Ramji, the junior-most member of the committee, finally spoke. He had just been demobbed from service in the Army and newly joined the committee. Respectful but ambitious, and unimpressed by commerce, in a quiet but confident voice, he said in English, 'Sahib, the building is the Ladies and Gents toilet.'

Lokbandhu

HE SAID HIS NAME was unimportant. It was what the people had begun calling him that was important, that was his name now. They called him Lokbandhu, the brother of the people. He was a perennial in our part of the civil service housing estate. He could be seen there when offices had closed, but also during all working hours. The ungenerous saw him as one of the unemployed, undeserving of alms. He himself felt that there was no employment in this backwater of Empire that he could condescend to, given the part that he had already played in the real struggle on the subcontinent.

When he had suddenly turned up near us, in 1949, he told us the British had forced him into exile, first in Tanganyika three years ago, and then here in Nairobi, just like Bahadhur Shah, the last Moghul Emperor who had been sent off to Rangoon in Burma, there to waste away and die. Did they not send away the Kabaka Daudi Chawa to exile in the Seychelles? Or Sultan Bargash from Zanzibar to Bombay? This is what the British did with all real patriots; inevitably, therefore, this had been his fate too. The papers which he had been forced to carry from the Bombay High Court at Ahmedabad in 1946 stating that an adjudication of bankruptcy had been made in regard to him, relating to unsatisfied execution warrants 'herewith attached, in the District Sessions civil cases enumerated below', only showed how exceedingly cunning the British were.

We knew that he had suffered under those British. When he had been a *satyagrahi*, he had been injured in the police *lathi* charges at every public meeting. But he and all those next to him had stood firm day after day. They had not retreated. They always took the blows, they had suffered. They never hit back. Such retaliatory violence would destroy the moral struggle. Gandhi would have been there, somewhere to the right of them. He was always with them. They were resisting the British. Lokbandhu was resisting the British. The British would have to go.

In the struggle, Lokbandhu said, he was always in white *khaddar*, cloth made from the spinning wheel of his mother at home, as taught by Bapu. 'Your mother knew *Bapu?*' we cried out. He assured us that that was not an issue. Bapu knew all his soldiers, and their families, and his family had long been one of them. They all knew Bapu, they were together all the time. During Satyagraha their white caps were visible everywhere.

'But why don't you wear *khaddar* here also?' we would ask. When he was brought here, the British—because they knew from their informers that the mere sight of him in the homespun would ignite Kenya—had taken away his white *khaddar*. The city would otherwise have turned into a cauldron of anti-British agitation.

The British had also put him in prison several times. They had read the depth of his patriotism. He was ready. He always remembered what his father had said when Lokbandhu, then aged sixteen, had told his father he was going to leave home to follow Gandhi and asked for his father's blessing.

His father had called him before the whole family and said, 'You have told us you are leaving home to follow Gandhiji. This is the right path, a noble path. Go with my blessing. But you must follow the path to the end. When you are beaten, when you are imprisoned, when you are tired, do not come back here to my house and say you cannot go on. I will turn you out of my house.'

We were deeply stirred by this. Though we did not invite our fathers to give us such a mixed blessing, we secretly thought less of our fathers for nevertheless not having issued it to us at all.

The British knew what a powerful orator he was. They had smarted under the lash when he had been a member of the Central Legislative Assembly in Delhi. True, he was participating in an imperialist institution, for that is what it was, but he was nobody's lackey. He had berated the Viceroy and the other members in the latter's Council for betraying the poor of India. Those traitors were only there to stay freedom's advance and help to lock up the leaders of the struggle. He too was ready, he told Mr Speaker, Sir, 'to go to prison for the millions of India, who are supported by the whole world except Britain. The time had come for the offensive flag above this chamber to come down. Forever. And a new flag, the flag of free India, to rise, never to come down. A flag that would be raised on this very building, and the Member for Law would then remember what he had said here today…'

We too wanted to be such orators against an unjust government, and we would pore over the bits that our teachers gave us from the wartime speeches of Winston Churchill, blissfully unaware of the irony.

The pen, Lokbandhu taught us, was mightier than the sword. We were overcome. This was heroic. Apart from being that, at last we Form III weaklings had an answer when the school toughs were around. It was no wonder Lokbandhu had been brought to court so often in India. That is always how the British, who spoke loudly about press freedom in England, actually dealt with patriot journalists in India and Kenya. Readers everywhere in India had read his columns in *The Times of India* and in *The Hindu* and in *The Statesman*. The police had come to take him away in handcuffs. Everybody had seen this base violation of free speech, dignity, and freedom.

We too wanted to be such patriots and writers who shook tyranny and exposed injustice. We would relate Lokbandhu's stories excitedly to our parents. But they only said disparaging things about him. We refused to believe them.

When we completed school and went away to university and studied things like law and political science and history, not a few of us had occasional thoughts of Lokbandhu.

I returned many years later, as a trained journalist. I sent in a few pieces that were run, and eventually I was accepted on the staff of, and began lowly courtroom reporting for, one of the dailies. Occasionally a short article would also be accepted. The sub often toned those down. One day I thought I saw Lokbandhu. I checked with my family about his whereabouts, and they said he was around. When I finally met him, he, of course, did not know me after all those years, but I reminded him of my school friends and how much we had all looked up to him, and how much we had enjoyed listening to him. I asked him as a favour, because of his extensive experience, to look at one of my pieces. It was on the direction the country was taking after the acceptance by KADU, the Kenya African Democratic Union, in 1962, to form a minority government. I had interviewed one of my father's friends who was among those who had taken office. I left the article with Lokbandhu and asked him to check it through. I would collect it whenever it was convenient. He hesitated, then said he would drop it off at my house, he knew our place.

I kept working on the piece but resolved to incorporate Lokbandhu's comments as soon as they came in, and then to submit it to my editor.

I was shocked therefore one morning to see my article appear in the paper, and worse, shown as having been authored by Lokbandhu.

I rushed to the editor's office. 'What is this? What is this?' I cried as, pages open, I burst through his door. He interrupted the reading of his mail and glanced casually at the page I thrust before him. 'Yes,' he said, 'it seemed a reasonable viewpoint, worth putting to our readers. And I liked that interview, nobody had got that party before.' He misread my injured look. 'I must say, it was better than anything he has been bringing in the past.'

'But...but,' I spluttered, 'It's mine. It's my article. I wrote it. It's mine! It's mine! I gave it to him to look at. Where is he? I want to see him!'

There was silence. Then the editor burst out laughing. 'No wonder,' he managed between continuing peals of laughter, 'no wonder he wanted his payment so quickly. He said it was to pay for his fare. I don't think you'll be seeing him. He left for India the day before yesterday.'

Room No. 8, Law Courts

ROOM NO. 8 was actually two rooms: the first was the open area flanked by the long counter the length of the room. This was filled with the Judiciary's clerks, court clerks, the judges' clerks, accountants, interpreters not needed that day in court, diarists, messengers bringing in files, messengers taking out files. On the other side of the counter were the public, outnumbered by a scrum of advocates' court clerks, a pair of court reporters, and sometimes advocates themselves. All of these leaned throughout the day's office hours on the sturdy counter seeking to file papers, urgent and not so urgent, read files, have pleadings and letters stamped, pay court fees, collect receipts, and have documents signed by the Deputy Registrar and sealed by the Head Clerk.

To us, the seal was a huge piece of iron machinery, comparable in our short experience only to the railway bridge over the Nile at Jinja.

Its handle was a broad revolving bar that stood higher than us. When we thought Mr Tanna, the Head Clerk, was not looking, we would screw it down and then swing on the handle as it spun back to the top. We would look in the wastepaper baskets for discarded blue papers with 'Judicial Department' letterheads. We would collect broken green file tags. These were the very sinews of this great building, for no file could stay together without them, as it would soon become an unmanaged mass of disorganized paper. This would bring imperial supremacy into question. For an Empire's paper of record could never be kept other than in an organized file. A file of unmanaged documents was the hallmark of peoples who could not rule themselves. So for want of a green tag indeed an Empire could be lost. All over the Empire and therefore all over the world, the same green tag kept all files in fine order, and in those years, the sun never set on a loose file or, therefore, on that Empire.

The memoranda noted by all officers in the files were written with identical pens dipped in identical inkwells in identical wooden ink stands on their desks. The inks were sent out in heavy porcelain bottles, more suited to the produce of chemical factories than the needs of meticulous judgments. A member of the subordinate staff would go round the building replenishing the small inkwells in their stands. All writing was with penholders with replaceable nibs. There were no ball pens as yet. Government issue did not extend to fountain pens. Typewriters remained in the typing pool. So everyone took care of the tools of their profession: file covers, envelopes, letterheads, the tags, carbon papers, and porcelain inkwells, often chipped, and sometimes empty because broken. Our treasure hunts therefore were for the debris of these precious items, and our love of stationery remained long into our adult lives.

All these uniform cogs had to have a single buyer and a single distributor. For these were a miscellany of tried and tested tools for tried and tested systems. They were to provide for, and did go, simultaneously, to more than fifty countries of the Empire, to the high courts in Hong Kong, Kingston, Lagos, Georgetown, Kuala Lumpur, the Bahamas, St. Helena, and so on. This was done by the Crown Agents, the *dukawallas* of the Empire bureaucracy. As was pointed out by Stefan Zweig long ago, '…bureaucracy demonstrates its more than earthly power by staying the same forever. For any object within this sphere which is used up or worn out or lost is replaced by another identical object, requisitioned and delivered by the appropriate agency, thus providing the inconstant world with an example of the superiority of the powers that be.' And here these objects were reminders of the superiority of not just the bureaucracy, but of the Empire itself.

These identical items of these identical systems made it possible for the Judges of the Colonial Service to be posted to Fiji, and then five years later to Trinidad, and a further five years later to the Gold Coast. And report to work the next morning in an office with routines which were immediately familiar, accompanied by the identical clerical machine they had just left.

*

Room No. 8 was the nerve centre of the Supreme Court of Kenya (what we now call the High Court). It was one of the showcase buildings of colonial Kenya, replacing the original High Court building that had been put up in 1903, when a wood and corrugated iron structure had been considered an imposing structure. But after more than two decades, it had been called a 'tin' building, and a deteriorating one at that. Eventually a new and suitable building was duly opened on 8 May 1935. Now, in 1949, in the aftermath of the Second World War, Room No. 8 was situated in this paragon of imperialism.

The second part of No. 8 was a small room added to the long room. This was where the Executive Officer and the Chief Cashier of the Registry sat attending to the most intransigent queries and to the more important callers, such as the Registrar, the Deputy Registrars, and, often, the Judges and sometimes even the Chief Justice. However, the two tables did not exhaust the space. Behind these two tables was another door leading to another 'room'.

This other room was called the 'Civil Deposit,

the Supreme Court of Kenya at Nairobi'. But we knew better. It was a huge and dark cavern, it was mysterious, it was a Mabel Lucie Attwell Arabian Nights illustration made real. Every afternoon, we two cousins came from our nearby primary school and loitered around my father's table to be taken home after work. And we would see this room.

We knew that, really, it was Ali Baba's cave. For the room behind the Executive Officer was not a room for more clerks. It was a safe. It was a safe the size of a room. It was a strong room. In it were kept the files of scandalous cases, court exhibits, guns, bows and poisoned arrows, account books, bloodstained clothes, and, only incidentally, money.

It was strictly off limits to us, but often the door was open for hours on end. We would gaze in. Sometimes we would run in and frighten ourselves by fearing the door would suddenly clang shut, unheeding of our screams. And we would only be able to hammer at an unyielding steel wall till, exhausted, we would fall dead, while life continued on the other side, unknowing and uncaring of what had happened to us. Not unter-rified, we would then rush out.

*

Mr Bansi Lall, the Chief Cashier, was co-custodian of this safe. His superior, Mr Sturridge, one of the Deputy Registrars, was the other keeper of the keys with access to the contents of the safe.

Mr Bansi Lall was the one who opened it every morning. He it was who locked the door at the end of each working day. He locked it, then reopened it. Opened the huge heavy door again and shut it, locked it, and tried it again to satisfy himself that it had indeed been locked.

Then his subordinates followed Mr Bansi Lall out. He locked Room No. 8's main doors, and then the whole group walked into the long corridors and to the short stairs leading to the street. Outside they took only a few steps forward when Mr Bansi Lall would call out, 'Wait.' Then he would pat his waistcoat pockets, turn around and re-enter the building. The others would smile. Then follow him back to Room No. 8. He would reopen the main door of Room No. 8 and go to the inner room. There he would stand before the safe door and try the handle several times. Then draw out his key chain, select the key, and, inserting it carefully in the safe, open the big door. Silently, he would look over the mute files and items to ensure nothing had been taken since he had locked up a few minutes earlier. He would then shut the safe door again and slowly turn the key. He would again try the locked door several times.

Then they would all go back to Room No. 8's main door, head to the stairs, and walk out of the building again. A few steps later, Mr Bansi Lall would stop again. He would pat his waistcoat pocket slowly. Nobody would say a word. They would simply all turn with him and go in again to repeat the long check. Emerging from the building a third time, they would finally proceed homewards. Mr Bansi Lall had repeated this process every work day for all the twenty-three years he had been in charge of the keys.

*

One Monday morning, when all in Room No. 8 had arrived at work and were about to open the doors to the public, Mr Bansi Lall, as usual, opened the large safe door. He looked in to check that all was as he had left it the Saturday afternoon before. Then, in the sight of two clerks, his big frame dropped to the floor in a faint.

When the cry went up and all rushed in to attend to Mr Bansi Lall, they found a body and blood on the floor of the safe. The police were immediately called. Very soon, the room was swarming with people—the CID squad, the Registrar, even a curious Judge or two, many staff members from all over the building—all looking on at this incomprehensible situation. The body had been immediately identified. It was that of Mr Dyke-Acland. He was one of the accountants in the Accounts Department on the third floor, a man recently arrived from England.

For the rest of the week, there was a pall of silence over the whole building. Work went on quietly, and the Indian and African staff spoke to each other in hushed tones. They went about their duties with the shared unspoken thought that it was somehow the fault of somebody somewhere from their two communities. We blamed ourselves because these whites did not do terrible things like this to each other. Only we did.

The CID, more knowing of the internal disputes and rivalries within the Settler community, were not totally surprised by the event, but were certainly intrigued by the locked safe. Out of our sight, the sight of subject persons, they carried out a discreet but thorough investigation into the world of the white officers in the building. This was a world to which we were of course not privy, nor were we entitled to receive rumours from it. Chinese walls divided us all, even though we worked together every day for hours. The CID inquiries revealed an association between Mr Dyke-Acland and the young wife of Mr Sturridge.

By the following week, the police were able to piece together what they thought were the probable events. Sturridge had asked Dyke-Acland to see him the previous Saturday, then a half working day, in Room No. 8 after hours. There had taken place a reckoning that culminated in the shooting of Mr Dyke-Acland. Mr Sturridge had coolly opened the safe, dragged the body inside, and locked the safe, then Room No. 8. And disappeared.

This latter news caused the event to linger even more months in the small talk of our small civil service world, in which our families met claustrophobically all the time, at work and out of it in our housing estates. The event defined the year, like too many weddings in a neighbour's family or the arrival of a new Governor, something to be remembered in the following years even if we did not talk about it anymore.

Mr Sturridge had indeed disappeared. As had Mrs Sturridge. The government never found Sturridge. But then it did not try too seriously. To trace, bring back, and convict a white man for the murder of another white man was a bad precedent to set before a watchful population seeking similar treatment for whites who killed natives. There were not a few in this category, and not unoften either. The mandarins surrounding the Governor considered the matter. They were, they said always, the ones who 'understood Africa'.

They were long-time residents of Africa, they knew more than London about how to deal with conduct like this. It was a poor example to those they ruled. 'It is best,' they intoned, 'to allow time to move the whole episode into the oblivion of a short public memory.' And so, floor, safe, and scandal were all quickly cleaned up.

Mr Bansi Lall also disappeared. But more properly. He never recovered fully from the shock. He applied immediately for retirement, and soon thereafter left Kenya and went back to Jullundur, his family roots, and tranquillity.

My cousin and I never entered the fearful safe again.

A Loss

ON THE HIGH SPURS of the monsoon waves of the Indian Ocean, the big steamer shuddered and slid in a barely onward direction. They were in the middle of the ongoing storm. The deck was awash, the rain coming in low at them, laterally from out of the blanketing night darker for the horizons of cloud that had surrounded them the preceding twenty-four hours. The dim points on this partially enclosed deck no longer qualified as light. Shadows dripped off every bulkhead. Outside one end in the corner, the spirals of the crew's metal staircase faced out to sea, black turns in the ship's iron frame.

The enraged ocean had kept away any passenger movement on the deck. The lounges, the bars, and the dining room had already been closed and locked the past nights. In the dining room all the tables had been bolted to the floor. All other furniture that could slide down and back with bone-breaking force as the ship pitched and heaved had been removed down to the luggage holds. All glasses, bottles, and cutlery that could shatter, splinter, and cut had been stored. And as the big vessel moved down and up, rolled, and tossed about, nothing inside or on deck could remain in one place and horizontal.

With each wave the ship rose, engines turning at full steam ahead in a search for such traction as it could steal in this struggle. As the ship broke through the wave and fell nose first into the trough, the stern rose into the air, and the engine screws, now turning unharnessed against no opposition, were quickly shut off so that they would not race and break themselves into pieces. Then as the ship started another climb at the bottom, the engines were started again at full. In the alternate roar of the slam of the long slide to the bottom of the wave and the returning power, the darkness and the noise brought all human watch to blindness.

Two figures appeared on the spiral staircase open there to the elements. Emerging from below deck into the dark rain, they kept pausing in unsure balance on the edges of the narrow steps, large shards of the rain breaking in pieces over them. They waited briefly, swaying in the buffeting gale, their hold uncertain on the damp handrail. From the rise of this corner, the man's look swept the area: no passengers, no crew or officers could be seen.

He was short and thin. His name was Foolabhai Patwarlal. He was a second-class passenger from below. He was travelling with his family from Mombasa to Bombay. He was a shopkeeper. Of rations and the rest of a *duka's* eclectic merchandise, carrying on trade in an Indian residential area of Nairobi. He was a shopkeeper of means. But none of these means were visible in his usual appearance, clothes, possessions, or speech. The last of these rarely omitted a mention of his crippling poverty and his humble origins.

The family was travelling to India in the wedding season of 1952 for the marriage of the eldest boy. And hopefully also to make a bespoken arrangement for the future marriage of his daughter, who was now sixteen. This was the slight figure beside him on those spiral steps.

He was looking forward to the son's wedding and the ceremonies accompanying it. The clothes and ornaments of the women on his side had been obtained months earlier. The burden of the other costs of the wedding now lay on the bride's house. The bride was from the same small part of upper Gujarat as he had come from long ago. The dowry had been negotiated through the elders of both sides. He had since been pleasurably anticipating its receipt. Those negotiations had been long and tedious. But tedious negotiation was his strength. He could, with no change of expression, change his promises, his assurances, and any hints of having concluded parts of the agreement or figures, then hold out for a newly minted higher figure in serial tediousness. This had been his strength for decades as a trader and had been the foundation of his wealth. As well as, conversely, the principle of his insignificant charitable donations.

In those wedding negotiations of the previous year with the elders, he had also sought a future match for the girl. They had visited several families of their persuasion. They had been fortunate with the son. On the son, the man was making a real profit. And there were two younger boys to follow. Each would result in an income to him. But not so with the girl. The girl was a loss. Every elder they had sounded out, every family they had visited, had sought a dowry. He had proposed figures, then reluctantly raised them to another small sum. All these responses had been to counter demands which always seemed exorbitant to him. Such sums, in his view, would wipe out all that the boy's forthcoming marriage would bring him. His eyes lit up every time he thought of the latter.

But in the months prior to the travel, he had kept thinking that the girl, in contrast, seemed only a liability. When he entered the columns in the ledger of his children's worth, she would not show such a profit, only be an inevitable drain on his fortune. She would bring about the breaking of his lifelong and unwavering rule: never to part unprofitably with any portion of his money. He had not amassed it to give it away. He was not known for his contributions to the community's small dispensary or for his donations to famine relief in his village in India, when need arose. The girl, a thin figure, would in two years' time require him to make major debit entries in that set of account books that he maintained in his mind. Such a step had been unthinkable all his working life. Even if such a payment were avoided, but they found no husband for her, she would become a call on his purse for the rest of his life. He had seen this happen to other families in the community.

In the dark, through the storm's thunder and the blinding rain, he again looked around the empty corner and the exposed steps. He still saw no movement, no inquiring presence, no voice or look. Silently with one hand he undid her feeble hold on the hand rail, while his other grasped an unresisting ankle. In a single motion he pushed the slight weight over the handrail into the darkness. He did not know whether the sound he heard was the scream of the protesting engines, a sharp crack of thunder, or the cry of someone who had loved him.

Karatina

I REMEMBER TRAVELLING over rutted roads and heavily wooded byways towards an isolated destination in the mountain forest above Karatina. I remember that last holiday before Central Province erupted. I was eleven, it was August 1952, and the school holidays had started. We were on the annual family holiday, accommodated in someone else's car rather like steerage passengers on past ships were, filling not seats, but vacant spaces and corners or the tops of baggage or the sides of persons or the laps of elder siblings. We were oblivious of comfort or discomfort, only excited always by the journey itself, a frame of mind I hope I have retained the rest of my years.

The cars too would give us misleading assurances of reliability or comfort. After Nairobi's outskirts, Ruiru, and Thika, as we began climbing through the beautiful countryside, our loud exuberance at the holiday would be silenced whenever steam would suddenly erupt from under the front bonnet, with yet more overheating of the engine. All the cars would stop. The stationary offending car looked shamefaced. The ladies would quickly bring out the food they had packed for the journey. It would be shared around with warm soft drinks which were opened with cheers from us. We children loved these halts, but the men stood by anxiously, not sure whether this was not a major breakdown after all. Water would be poured into the hot radiator. After a while we would pack in again and move on.

An occasional Public Works Department diversion would lead us into country lanes with which we were unfamiliar. Improvising our way along, we would ask the few figures we crossed for confirmation of direction, for distance. 'Not far, just here,' they all said. Each pointed vaguely in the direction we were moving, even if it was the opposite of where we should have headed. It would be many, many different turns and many miles and several hours later that we would actually motor into the inquired destination or point of meeting, crossroads, or some small clearing.

The answers we had received were inaccurate. They were a ritual response of courtesy, a mark of helpfulness even though the speaker did not necessarily know the answer. We too were not offended or surprised if the directions proved inadequate or plainly erroneous. For did we too not come from a sub-continent which responded so when strangers asked for directions? Travellers there had over centuries observed that we thought that if such answers were not given, we 'would be failing in our duties of hospitality towards the stranger, and so made up directions even when we did not know them'. Thus, when finally we children disembarked from crowded backseats or the open rear of a pickup, we were shaken only by the unceasing jolting of the corrugated murram roads, the adults more by the constantly dashed expectation of imminent arrival.

We stopped at Saba Saba, then a single lane off the road, to greet one of our passengers' aunts married there, drawing up at her husband's *duka*. More soft drinks followed this pleasurable reunion. We would enter Fort Hall with relief, to replenish fuel and with the assurance of acquaintances there. Then on to Sagana, there to watch with awe the workings of the large factory of Seth Premchand Vrajpal.

To travel such distances was rare and great adventure. At that time for us urban children of Nairobi, travel in a car was not common. Few of our families owned one. Yet, though we did not know any rich people, we did know many generous people who shared. And so from time to time we did sit in a car. For us then, to be taken in a car to the centre of the city was travel, to Athi River was to reach the rim of the horizon, and to Dagoretti Corner was to come dangerously close to the edge of the world. These trips set landmarks in our memory.

On the way to Karatina, moving up Pole Pole Hill when it was a murram road was a set of ex-pectations rather than any assurance of passage. Doing so in underpowered, overloaded cars with drivers unfamiliar with it was adding handicap weights upon a weak contender. I remember when we reached the top, all the cars pulled up on one side of the road, not by reason of any mechanical breakdown. It was for the drivers to draw breath as if the car had been a cart they had been pulling and pushing up, and to regain their composure, which the anxiety of the very steep hill had sharply dislodged.

We reached Karatina as the sun weakened, arriving at the town house of our host, Dara Khan, the family of timber merchants and transporters with a logging concession and a sawmill higher up in the forests above Karatina. We called him Uncle. The lovely large house was an extensive log cabin set in a green clearing beside a quick stream.

The excitement of the day, and parents, soon sent us off to bed after an abundant highland meal. Hours later, I am still awake, the invigorating air and the newness keeping sleep away. The stream sounds clearly in the silence. An occasional lorry labours its way up the hill, straining through the gears. Creaks descend from the roof as the wooden house stretches.

'Visitors. Go. Here are some. Go.' I think it is Uncle. There is a low response, then Uncle says 'Tomorrow.' The urgent whispering outside stops. I do not even hear movement.

In the morning there is a huge breakfast. Then, accompanied by Uncle, one of his brothers, and some of their staff, we set out in a convoy of our cars and their trucks. Now we drive up the mountainside, deep into the forest. After an hour we hear a high-pitched drilling sound, announcing that we have reached the sawmill and logging site. There are many cabins, stores, the mill, more lorries, and, scattered over, the iron debris of busy operations. This is where we will stay for the next four days. The elders would also do some hunting.

When we woke up the following morning, it was much colder than Karatina. The trees green and huge around us, then rising darker and distant, the forest's edges rose nebulously into a white peak.

Two days later we accompanied Uncle down into town. Town was not the treat. Standing in a big moving lorry was. Uncle tells one of the drivers, as the latter moves to the cab, 'No, I will take it myself.' All of us pile into the open back of the lorry with one of Uncle's brothers. In town, Uncle drives to the provision store. 'Patel Sahib, we have guests, what have you got today?' He does a large amount of shopping, with several sacks of cabbages, potatoes, and other items loaded on to the lorry. While all this is being done, we walk down the street with Uncle to the Post Office to clear his post box. There he has long, cordial chats with Settler friends he meets outside. Before we leave in the lorry, we go to the petrol station and fill the tank.

We drive back to the town house. There a few of the sacks which we had purchased are unloaded and taken into the garage workshop. After a while, Uncle and his brother emerge carrying one of these sacks. Some of us run up to help carry it. But Uncle shakes his head and sends us off. They carry one more of these from the workshop and load them on the lorry, joining the other sacks still there. We are called to jump on, and we head up to the logging site; this time Uncle is with us in the back of the lorry, and his brother is driving.

As we move higher up the mountainside, Uncle stands at the rear next to the open tailgate. After a while we are on tracks that do not seem to be the way we had come down that morning.

Occasional planks of wood are nailed to the trees. They carry a number and the initials F.D. A faded wooden board appears, explaining, 'Forest Department'. There is no sign of people or livestock.

As we begin lurching through a narrow and sharp corner, rising higher, a sack falls off. I look up at once at Uncle. But he does not look back. He is looking around carefully into the forest all around us. A few yards away, as the turn enters a particularly bad rise of pointed rocks, the already slow vehicle stops to change down into first gear. At the tailgate I notice the toe of Uncle's boot move under the other sack with a sharp heave. The second sack falls off. It hits the points of the rocks, rolls down roughly, and lands on the first sack several feet below where the corner started. Both sacks tear, potatoes pour out of the second sack and cabbages out of the first. But among the cabbages, two sticks of metal poke out, then gleaming wood. I see the guns. I involuntarily raise my hand immediately, pointing at the sacks and looking at Uncle. He ignores me into silence,

and the lorry jerks forward in fits as the gear en-
gages noisily and slowly gathers purchase. After a
while, looking anxiously around, Uncle pulls up
the tailgate.

We are surprised when we suddenly reach the
cabins we had left in the morning. We have used
another route. 'Now for some food,' Uncle cries
heartily as he jumps down from the lorry, then
speaks aside in whispers with his brother.

We spent another day in that idyll, running
up and down the mountainside, occasionally
moving out from among the great trees into a
clear view of the gleaming peak even higher and,
though close, always remote from us.

We drove down the next evening to the town
house, from where we would leave the following
morning for the return to Nairobi. But I had
something to do first. I had over those days been
wondering whether I had imagined the voices I
had heard the first night. Yet I had also seen the
sacks on the mountain. Had it really been Uncle's
voice that I had heard the first night? Before
dinner, I casually make my way alone to behind

my bedroom, between its rear wall and the thick kai apple hedge that is the property's fence. I see nothing unusual. I search the ground and bits of the hedge, but find nothing. I move away.

*

I met Uncle again decades later. He was now a publicly acknowledged patriot and a hero of the independence struggle. Within months of our holiday visit, the Emergency had been declared, on 20 October 1952. He had been tracked, he had been arrested. Evidence had been gathered against him. But the British had not charged him with any offences. He had known these carried the death penalty. Possession of bullets, the giving of them to those labelled 'terrorists', the supply of food to the gangs in the forest, the consorting with them, the supply of guns to them were by that time all capital offences.

But the British knew that bringing him to trial on these grave offences would only show to the world that the Mau Mau movement and its armed struggle had broader support than just the

Kikuyu, Embu, and Meru communities; that this was not just a Kikuyu war, but a countrywide rejection of British rule, and that the Kikuyu army in the forests and camps carried with its intense determination and bravery a large part of the rest of the country, including this Pakistani Kenyan.

For their forbearance, the British devised other punishment for him. It was as devastating to him. He was to go into exile. And they imposed also a fine—the fine of silence.

He had been out for years till freedom returned to Kenya. After that, when young persons met him they would gather around him and ask him how he had fought the British, what he had done, and the dangers he had faced. But the decades had taken their toll. Now he had forgotten the details of his heroism. The memories, the facts of particular incidents, and the chronology of his bravery had leached away. In his mind the bigger battle had been to handle the choices that he had been making day after day, night after dangerous night. What I had seen that long-ago holiday had been only the immediate prelude to what followed once the Emergency had been formally declared in the October that followed. Every moment of every day had then carried the need to fend off impending danger, to remove signs of guilt, to keep lines of supply ongoing, to sustain the camouflage of old friendships with the enemy, while yet aiding this sharp thrust for freedom and dignity.

His heroism had been the instinctive rejection of oppression. It was fed by the pride of demolishing the racism of the oppressors. But coping was not one set battle, one event, capable of being retold as such. It was a series of anxieties, unending days and sleepless nights of doubts, of putting loved ones in danger, and fear. These were the ratchet turns that did not lend themselves to recall or narrative.

For coping was facing, adjusting to fear, the process of which was the true bravery. And to the imminence of loss. When the outcome is winning or losing honourably, we call it 'a brave act'. But for him it had not been one act to win or lose. It had been a long, testing process. It was something different from what others now praised him for, or what they researched, or what they thought he had 'done'. For him, it had not been events, but an inchoate period in his life. There was no one arrival at winning, losing, or resolution. It had grown out of how he had wanted to live, not accepting injustice or repression. His actions had emerged out of this, and he had never expressed any of this in words as he had continued to go about his day-to-day family and business matters. From this had come a sequence, perhaps many, of conclusions and actions spread over those many years in the task of subverting colonial rule and racial arrogance, which had reinforced each other into a daily living full of danger for him.

But these now, the years after Independence, were new times, full of different hopes. Now the country was drawing away from that past. Even those who knew what he had done became engrossed in new goals, bringing silence to the past.

So when the young persons asked him what he had done, he said, 'Yes, we fought them', or 'You know they came for me', or 'We had to', but those years had faded from recall. He could no longer recite the narratives of suspense, bravery, and heroism that these young persons so wanted to hear.

But I knew a little part of it. It was a part I came to realize and put together over long years, through doubtful recall, pieced together by checks with those I found later who knew what he had done and also with those who had shared that eventful holiday. Then, I knew, I had been witness to bravery for freedom and dignity in my own future.

Meet with Food

DEPARTURES FROM Mombasa Railway Station were always festive occasions for the community. They were social obligation, business opportunity, and inexpensive entertainment all in one. The whole of the extended families of the four students travelling had of course come to see them off. Showing them support were also numerous family friends, the community heads with their wives and families, and their hangers on, present to affirm their usefulness at all times. With the latter were their acquaintances who had nothing else to do that evening. Platform tickets then were ten cents each.

The women had dressed specially for the evening. They had also carefully supervised the dresses, footwear, and very discreet glitter of their young daughters. Long before the train left, they were all in animated conversation. The fathers of the four, with the community seniors and colleagues from the office, stood on another side, conversing in subdued tones. This conveyed, in contrast with the other noisy conversations, that theirs was of important matters. From time to time Ramesh's father, who worked in the Booking Office, disappeared to tell the guard, or the catering and bedding staff, to keep an eye on the boys, who were to occupy the four berths in their second-class compartment courtesy of staff concessionary rates.

The mothers kept a special eye on the boys who were to travel, while routinely admonishing the younger children who ran about on a platform long familiar to them. As departure time approached, the mothers fussed the four boys on board, and made sure they each had the dinner that their respective mothers had prepared for them. Oil-stained brown paper bags or newspaper wraps tied with string identified these. The younger children had been pulled away from the edge of the platform even before the guard's whistle had trilled readiness to depart. The engine's deep whistle had then blown. The chorus of goodbyes was uninterrupted by the train's clanging start; it pulled away slowly.

That month, December, the school year had ended and they had completed Form Three. In January of the next year, 1954, they would go into Form Four and, at the end of that year, sit for their Cambridge examinations. They were now on their annual railway holiday upcountry. They had done this since Form One, when they had discovered that their fathers all worked for the East African Railways and Harbours.

Before the train had departed, they had walked up the platform to look into the dining car from the outside. In the tradition of restaurant cars, it was a named bogie carriage, called *Longonot* after the dormant volcano in the Rift Valley. They had jumped up and down several times on the platform to catch brief glimpses of gleaming glasses, polished spoons, and starched tablecloths on the as yet vacant tables. They had returned to their coach and boarded it full of anticipation about the plan they were going to implement.

None of them had enough money to eat dinner in the restaurant car, but they had long felt that they must know what it was like. So, in school, they had decided that on this trip they would pool their rationed funds for one day, and one of them would go for dinner in the restaurant car. Then another one would do the same on the return trip. Fazal had won the calls when they had tossed a coin to decide who would be the one on this Up trip. He was excited by the forthcoming treat.

The train passed Mazeras. Looking constantly out of the window, their hair had blown stiff and their eyes hurt from the occasional smuts that flew at them from the smoke of the engine. Darkness had fallen when they finally heard the sound of the dinner gong coming down the corridor for the second time. They had been allocated a card and a seat in this second sitting, not being privileged enough to qualify for the first sitting. As the waiter passed, sounding a pleasant scale on the small xylophone, Fazal went out of the compartment.

He moved down the swaying corridor and crossed over to the next carriages, giving way to the porter in one, and in another, squeezing past people still at the corridor windows. The pleasant aroma of cooking told him he had reached. He entered and stopped, balancing against the movement of the carriage. The warm and subdued lighting fell on wood panelling the length of the carriage. The end panels exhibited photographs of views from the extensive railway system—large sepia photographs of the Nile Bridge with a train going over it, a double-headed goods train climbing laboriously to the summit of the Rift Valley, a lake steamer standing alongside bales of cotton at Kisumu Pier, a young couple at a coupé window pointing out a pair of giraffe to their excited child. Fazal had grown up with such photographs, enclosed in broad wooden frames, adorning the offices where his father worked.

Before him was the spread of spotless white linen, inscribed silverware, and monogrammed plates, laid out in formation, table after table. He looked at the first table. Filled with pleasure, he thought, 'This is what we had been dreaming about.' At that moment the Chief Steward came up to him, dressed in a stiff white uniform.

'Your card?' he said, putting out his hand. Fazal said, 'What?' and simultaneously answered him by handing over the card. The Chief Steward looked at it and said, 'Here,' and took him to a table further down, partly occupied, and pointed to a vacant seat.

Fazal sat down next to a Sikh man, and then lifted his gaze. On his left, across the very narrow aisle, three persons were dining at the table. The two men did not look up or interrupt their conversation. They had reddish faces, were broadly built, and wore blazers. Facing them was a blonde woman. As Fazal sat down, she turned and courteously smiled across at him as he joined the dinner. Fazal froze. The Chief Steward moved away. Fazal looked down. He had never before had such a neighbour at a meal.

The steward, also dressed in white, came up, placed down freshly sliced bread, moved various items about efficiently, and expertly placed the soup plate in between the rocking cutlery and glasses. Fazal glanced up in panic. The lady, still smiling, had rejoined the conversation at her table. Fazal's face flushed. Fazal had never eaten food while persons such as these were near him. Now they were right next to him. He could not eat in their presence. His hand ceased movement. It would not pick up the spoon. Several moments passed. He remained looking down. The soup lay untouched. He could not eat in their presence.

With forced and awkward movements, he made himself get up. Without looking at the table across or at any of the tables he was passing, he fled very slowly out of the restaurant car. Passing the kitchen area, he became conscious that his face was flushed and that he was shaking. He continued till he came to the next passenger coach, and opened a corridor window. The moving air, cooler even though they were still not far from the sea, helped. What would he say to the others? What could he? He remained at the window.

'Hey, man?'

'Finished?'

'No,' Fazal muttered. 'No. No.' They asked many questions, but Fazal remained unexplaining. His incomplete sentences told the others nothing. The subject finally changed and they got onto their prepared bunks, welcomed by the fresh sheets and the warm blankets marked EAR & H.

Later in the night, Fazal leaned over the upper

bunk and whispered to Raymond. 'Hey, man, I'm hungry. Where's my packet?'

'Kalwant finished it before you closed the door as you went.' He heard Raymond's suppressed laughter, 'He likes your mother's food.'

Fazal sighed involuntarily. He had already returned the others' money. He lay back to sleep.

Unused to it, the chilly upland air in the dawn at Kima made them shiver, and they had to pull out their school sweaters from their unglamorous army surplus haversacks. They kept on their sweaters as they reached Nairobi, higher even than Kima.

This year their parents' friends were not meeting them at the station, as they were not to stay in Nairobi. They were to spend this holiday in Nakuru. But first, since they were passing through, a few days would be spent with Ramesh's uncle, the station master at the small station of Muguga, and then with an elder family friend, also a station master, at Escarpment Station a few miles on. From Nairobi they would therefore be catching the train onwards the same evening.

They got out of Nairobi Station into the big

parking lot, and walked down Government Road. On their left rose the imposing Railway Headquarters building. They were ignorant of the history it shared with them, ignorant that they were there in its wake. They did not think anything had brought them to this land. They were born in Mombasa, here, how could anything bring them to this land? Thus its redstone grandiloquence touched no chord in them. They knew nothing of the Raj. They had not ever been to India, nor had any of their fathers.

They wandered around the city through the rest of the morning. Towards the lunch hour, they headed to the small milk bar they had been told about. It belonged to a wrestler. This was the famous Dhaman Singh, son of Bhola Singh Bahra. They had heard of him. Dhaman Singh held matches and demonstration bouts at the various fairs and fêtes that took place in the colony. His *lassi* was equally famous, and the unspoken message it carried was that those who drank this drink of yoghurt and milk, garnished with sugar or salt, would also become as strong and successful as its maker. It was obvious to all his vociferous supporters that Dhaman Singh had achieved his position as a *pehlwan,* a champion wrestler, ready to take on all comers, and unbeaten by any, with the help of his famous drink. So the boys had his *lassi*, sitting on worn-out benches amid the many patrons in the small room. Fazal's ignominious defeat of the previous night slowly left his mind, becoming only another of such meetings. Then, by reason of the excellent taste, as well as by the unspoken hope that they would progress from their skinny selves to Dhaman Singh's stature, they had several more glasses of the drink.

After moving around the city in the afternoon, they returned to the station and rejoined the evening train to Kisumu. The train made its ponderous climb to Kikuyu. Here it stopped to replenish its water tanks. The next station was Muguga, but the train did not stop there. They were therefore to get down here, at Kikuyu Station, and spend the night at the house of Mr Kotecha, the station master, and proceed to Muguga in the morning. He helped the boys down and left them near the signal cabin while he attended to his duties. When the train left, he took them to his small house at the end of the station.

'They have come,' he called to his wife as he entered.

Mrs Kotecha knew neither the boys nor their parents. It was enough that they were the boys belonging to Mr Patel, the station master at the next station, Muguga, and needed to be taken care of for the night. All travellers were always welcome, and she had a duty to look after them. After they had washed, she placed metal plates and drinking vessels full of water on their small table while the boys looked on appreciatively. They had not eaten since the *lassi*. She brought two *sufurias* to the table and lots of bananas. She kept bringing freshly made chapatis. It was a simple meal, but there were enough chapatis, even for Kalwant, and he rose from the table not displeased. Soon the four of them were asleep on the floor of the narrow corridor in the small railway quarters.

In the morning they were up early, but had to wait for the Kisumu Down Mail to Nairobi to pass Kikuyu Station before they could start off. The train rushed in eventually, seemingly very fast for a train that was going to stop. But it did do so by the time the engine reached the end of the long platform. The windows were full of passengers, anticipating that they would soon be disembarking at their final destination, Nairobi. While urchins ran up and down selling boiled eggs, women sold maize and fruits as they moved steadily down the lower-class coaches, experienced at catching the eye of intending, or even hesitating, buyers.

After the train left, the boys returned to the small house to thank Mrs Kotecha. A grimy tank engine was shunting a few goods wagons back and forth as they said their goodbyes. No one had paid it any attention while the mighty and many-wheeled articulated Garratt mainline locomotive that had just departed with the Nairobi train had been present. Now the small engine's frequent short whistles made up for its discontent at always being bereft of admiration while the brightly painted Garratts roared all over the system looked upon by all with awe. Mrs Kotecha gave them a bundle of chapatis and some bananas, saying shyly, 'These are for you. There is no one to make you eat properly while you are there,' for she knew Ramesh's uncle at Muguga was unmarried.

They were to walk on the track to Muguga Station. It was five miles away. Mr Kotecha saw them off at the end of the platform. As they walked on the curve out of the station, they waded through the pools of water at the foot of the high water tower which serviced the tenders of the steam locomotives, and began their hike in a gentle climb. Below them on their left was a small lake. On the lake were cows, grazing serenely on the green that had now overcome most of the water. It was one of the lakes among the ridges there which periodically metamorphosed into meadow and then back again into water, another of the many miracles between Mombasa and Kisumu that this line offered to its passengers. Taking it for granted, as young persons do all miracles, they chatted on.

The rails soon entered woods. Their voices suddenly sounded loud in the silence of the high trees around them. From their edges, the downs of Muguga Agricultural Institute rolled away in front of the boys. The scene was a rich green with a distant frame of deep blue trees. The boys were strangers to this lush and fresh highland landscape. The landscape of their coastal home was dirty urban sand below stucco buildings, whose paint, constantly battered by an over-bright sun and scoured by aggressive salt-laden winds, had turned to a uniform non-colour which invited no admiration. Here, in contrast, the mock-Tudor building with dark timber and clean white plaster contrasts advanced its charms to this quartet of philistines, who kept walking on unheeding.

After more than an hour of walking, the rails crossed under the road bridge to Nakuru, one among the many recent changes to tidy up the line, which included the new alignment from Nairobi to Kikuyu. As they crossed under, they became conscious of a wind blowing incessantly at them. It came at them uninterrupted for fifty miles over the sweep of the Athi Plains, which they had passed the day before, till it reached this rising ground where they now were. They were looking at horizons with which they were not familiar at all.

They tramped in leisurely fashion on and off the sleepers between the rails. When a short goods train came busily from the direction of Limuru, they all clambered down the ballast onto the sides. The driver blew short blasts on the whistle in both warning and greeting, and the guard, knowing they would be walking up, waved at them as the train passed. It seemed to move quickly when next to them, but appeared to be very slow when it had passed them and was at a distance.

As they went along, Kalwant was the first to open Mrs Kotecha's thoughtful parcel, sharing out the spare contents. Eating slowly and talking much, they finally reached Muguga Station. There was only one office, and they immediately met up with Ramesh's uncle.

They spent the afternoon in the station precincts, lying on the grass on the other side of the station tracks. They were looking down in the distance at Nairobi city's few tall buildings. And much farther away at the bulk of Ol Donyo Sabuk, and the faint angle of Lukenya from whence their train from Mombasa had come.

They spent two days there and, contrary to Mrs Kotecha's well-intentioned expectations, ate delicious food in quantities that delighted Kalwant. The principal fare was chicken, cooked in a variety of dishes by Mr Patel's staff. This was his habitual but secret fare, for this was not what he could have asked any wife to prepare for him without earning opprobrium from both vegetarian families.

The third morning, they began walking from Muguga to Limuru Station, from which they would later catch an afternoon Up Goods to Escarpment Station. The line took them into open fields, the wind again blowing strongly at them. After a while, the line began curving around the sides of the hills that became frequent as it kept climbing. The boys, coastal inhabitants, were panting, unused to the air at seven thousand feet above their usual ground. Then as they marched on the sleepers to the next hill, the line did not turn with the contour, but instead went into a dark portal opened up in the side of the hill. This was Limuru Tunnel. They had been told about it. It too was part of the new alignment after the War. It had been bored, and the line ran, under a fine, conscientiously worked Settler farm. As they entered the tunnel, sudden cold air descended on them and they shivered. For them, the middle of the earth was not a hot inferno. It was a damp and chill hole, the sun and warm air left outside. They put on their torches and, as their eyes adjusted to the dark, moved carefully between the rails, keeping anxious ears and eyes open for the sound or light of any train. Their words began to echo briefly, and the boys enjoyed a few moments of shouting.

Eventually they saw a pin of light, but for a long while no opening seemed larger or nearer, until at last they seemed suddenly to walk out into the mid-morning's hot sun. They rounded a shallow lake and the station buildings came into view.

A few hours later, after a frugal but welcome lunch, they waited on the platform for the train that was to take them on to Escarpment Station up the line. It was the goods train, bound for Gilgil and from there diverting on to the branch line to Thomson's Falls. They would travel in the guard's van.

As they stood around, joined intermittently

by the station master, they saw trucks drive to the small pedestrian level crossing a few yards away in the direction of Nairobi. A troop of policemen jumped down. Dressed in long blue overcoats, with puttees and boots, they wore black army helmets. They broke into two single files and marched to the station, entering on either side of the second track at the station and taking up positions at its far end on both sides of that track.

In a short while an engine whistle was heard, and the goods train from Nairobi bundled into view and then into the station. It drew to a creaking halt on the second track.

The boys, who had been watching them, saw the policemen on both sides of the wagons commence a search, working their way from the wagons in the front to those at the back.

Suddenly, as the policemen reached midway, a door opened from the rearmost wagon. A figure appeared in the exit, struggling to jump out. The metal doors clanged loudly. Shouts went up from the policemen, who began running along the long train towards the wagon. The man jerked himself free and tumbled out. Seeing the policemen rush-ing towards him, he slid under the wagon to the other side, only to find the police file on that side running towards him.

The boys saw his feet stop, then swiftly turn to the guard's van, the final carriage. He moved past it and turned across it to make a break for the road beyond the station. He came into their view again as he moved to cross the first track.

Suddenly, and wholly unexpectedly, shots rang out from the direction of the road. The boys turned and saw that two blue police cars had appeared there. The man drew away from the platform fence and sped down the tracks in the direction from which the train had come. But ahead of him now, on the footpath crossing the tracks, the first truck and a group of officers waited to cut off his escape.

Too late the man saw the danger. He turned sharply to the left, hesitated. As the officers moved closer towards him, the fugitive looked around and then desperately ran back and mounted the platform again for its fence to the road.

The first shot caught him in the back, and as he spun, two more hit him. He fell on the platform, still.

Ramesh staggered involuntarily against the waiting room wall and threw up. The others remained in a huddle next to the office. Fazal's ashen face continued staring at the unmoving heap.

Their first dead man.

Mr Dave, the guard of the goods train, came up to them. 'Are you Patel's boys?' he asked, for this goods train was the very train they were to move on in. None of them answered him. Mr Dave laughed at their mute response. 'You don't know? He is Mau Mau. He had hidden lots of ammunition and guns in the wagon. He was taking them to Thomson's Falls for the forests there.'

They spent the next two days at Escarpment Station, subdued and unable to stop talking about what they had witnessed at Limuru.

Their final night there, they packed and got ready for moving on to Nakuru. The railway's official timetable said that the Nakuru passenger night train did not stop at Escarpment. But that night, when the train reached Escarpment, it slowed down, and made an unscheduled stop. Unauthorized telegrams had been exchanged between Ramesh's father in Mombasa and the Escarpment station master, their old family friend, also a Mr Patel, the contents of which had been passed on to the driver of the train.

When the train came to a creaking halt, old Mr Patel boarded the carriage. In unhurried but highly efficient fashion, he helped the boys up from the ground, and settled them in the compartment reserved for them. They said their goodbyes, and, descending from the carriage, Mr Patel swivelled his hand signal lamp glass to green and held up the light towards the engine. A short burst of steam, bright in the dark, from Mr Daljit Singh Pannu, the driver, acknowledged the communication, and within the minute, the train had pulled out from the empty station. Old Mr Patel's thirty-six years of service in the Railways had steadily turned what had started out as precarious employment in his youth into respect and a proud record. So that, always with discretion, in his time he had halted trains in this fashion for dukes, eminent hunters, secretaries of state, humble Settlers, Special Branch officers, visiting religious leaders from India, railway superiors, colleagues, and once even a prince. Driver Pannu would now easily make up the lost minute on the remaining part of the run down the escarpment to Longonot, Naivasha, and Nakuru.

That afternoon in his office, old Mr Patel had said to them, 'You will reach Nakuru at midnight tonight. I will tell them to collect you.' Kalwant had looked up, thought briefly, then said, 'Tell them to bring some food with them.' Old Mr Patel had smiled and tapped out, 'Boys arriving NRO at 2355 hrs on B07 Up. Meet with food.'

The boys waved their thanks to old Mr Patel into the darkness. They had a last shared holiday time ahead of them in Nakuru. There would be no such trip again.

*

Many decades later, Kalwant would say it was thus that he had become responsible for another addi-tion to the list of linguistically notable telegrams for which the railway's *babu* station masters had by then long been famous all over the English-speaking world.

Raymond, in remote Australia by then, would tell his children of his charmed school holidays when they used to walk on train tracks in the country for which his heart still ached. Ramesh returned from studies abroad to a routine which, whenever he had to move between Nairobi and Mombasa, allowed his busy businesses the time that only airplanes can take. After a while, he did not notice that his use of railway travel to his home in Mombasa had faded away.

In a quick turnaround, the handsome Fazal, in England ever since, was never again so unmanned. In those succeeding years, he never had to think of what had happened at that restaurant car meal.

'Tell Him'

KAMAU WAS SPEAKING to him in an urgent voice. Kamau had worked for him once. Now he was something in some political group that was spoken of all the time, but of which Purchand knew nothing. Kamau had still retained his connections with the shop and its regulars. And he met them all the time in and outside the shop.

Kamau was now impressing his words on him. 'You saw the man with the glasses?'

'Yes.'

'He is Murumbi.'

'Who?'

'From KAU. From the Kenya African Union.'

Purchand remained silent, uncomprehending.

'He has come here from the trial.'

'What trial?'

'Kenyatta's trial.' There was a pause. 'He is looking for witnesses.'

'About what?'

'Some people have been taken there to tell the court about the time Kenyatta came to Ol Kalou. You remember we saw Kenyatta two years ago here?'

'Oh, yes,' said Purchand.

It had been a major ripple in the stagnant waters of his life at Ol Kalou. That afternoon there had been a public meeting. Kenyatta had spoken. Purchand, of course, had not attended. But he had seen the great excitement that the visit had caused. Many policemen had come in the speaker's wake to the small centre.

That evening, Kamau had knocked on the back gate, and when Purchand had opened it Kamau had brought in the chairs that he had taken that afternoon to the bar for the meeting. As they were speaking, a small but animated group emerged from the rear gates of the bar, which faced Purchand's own rear gate. A broad man of medium height, in a leather jacket and carrying a walking stick, was at the centre of the small circle. He was talking spiritedly. Kamau had pointed to him. That is Kenyatta. Purchand had looked at him. He had no knowledge of what the man was doing, but he heard him spoken of as the leader.

Purchand and Kamau had looked on as the group had walked to a parked car. The car had then driven away down the lane to their left.

Purchand and Kamau had remained looking at the departing car, when a woman had appeared from the nearby field on their right. She had headed towards the bar. Kamau had greeted her. 'Who do you want?'

'Nobody,' she had said. But she had stopped.

Kamau had looked at her more closely, then had said, 'I know you. You are from Nakuru.'

She had not said anything.

'Yes?' Kamau had insisted.

She had simply nodded.

Kamau had said, 'You are at the Impala Bar there?'

Again she had remained silent.

'Rebeka?'

'Eeehh.'

'Wait,' Kamau had said, and had turned to Purchand, 'I will put these inside.' And started carrying in the chairs in pairs.

The woman had stood there patiently. When Kamau had put away the last of the chairs, he had returned and said to her, 'Come,' and they had walked together into the bar. That had been just over a year ago.

Now they were standing again at his gate opposite that bar yard, as Kamau pressed him. 'This is where we were, and the woman there?'

'Yes.'

'The woman has been taken to that trial. To Kapenguria. She is now saying in court that she was in this bar when Kenyatta was inside. She has told the court that she heard him saying bad things. She is saying that he was talking about oaths…'

At the last word, Purchand took in his breath sharply. He knew that was forbidden. Then slowly he said, 'But he had left before she came. We saw him go.'

'Exactly. That is what I told the man. You tell him.'

'How can I do that?' Purchand cried out. 'I don't know anything.'

'You saw Kenyatta go. You said so yourself just now.'

'Yes, but…'

'Kenyatta had gone before the woman even came to the bar, isn't that so?'

'Ye-e-es.'

'Then tell that to the man from Nairobi.'

'I don't know him.'

'You know what he is doing here.'

'He is against the government.'

'He is not against anybody. He is trying to find the witnesses to defend Kenyatta.'

'He is against the government.'

'He is trying to get the truth to that trial. He is trying to get anybody who knows what happened that day to tell that to the court.'

'I am not a witness. I have never been inside a court.'

'But you saw what happened.'

'I don't know.'

'You *do* know. This can save Kenyatta. You can save Kenyatta.'

'How can I save anybody?'

'You can. If you don't keep quiet. If you tell the man what you saw.'

As he spoke, Kamau kept looking to their right across the empty field at the main road fifty yards away, the direction from which the woman had come that time. From the Gilgil side on that road, a small group of blue station wagons now came at high speed. It was a police convoy. It stopped abruptly. Before Purchand could reply, Kamau pulled him into the shadows. His voice dropped to urgent whispers as he kept pressing Purchand.

'You must tell him. Don't keep quiet.'

'But I don't know this man.'

'I will send him to you.'

'No!'

'He will take your statement.'

'No, no. I have never written. They have told us not to help these bad people.'

Just the previous month, November, soon after the declaration of the Emergency, the police had called all the shopkeepers and warned them against assisting the Mau Mau with food or clothes, or sheltering them in their shops or homes. They were told not to sell items to such people.

'Bad people? Is old man Chege bad? Is Kinuthia bad?'

These were old friends and long-time sharers of time at the shop. In alarmed surprise, Purchand exclaimed, 'They are Mau Mau?'

Kamau did not answer him, then continued. 'Your people fought them in India.' Purchand nodded his head, and a faint response stirred feebly in a remote pinpoint in his body. It might have passed in some quarters as a patriotic feeling.

Kamau continued, 'Then why can't we fight them here? Are we not fighting the same enemy?'

Purchand had accepted British rule in India as his enemy, but could not comprehend British rule in Kenya as his enemy. Here he earned his livelihood under their rule. He had never considered Kamau's questions before.

'They will harm me. Bad… They will…' He could not think of the ultimate in harm that the police could do to him.

Suddenly, the blue vehicles that had stopped on the main road began moving again, quickly.

Some continued straight on the main road, but others turned in sharply onto the empty field towards them. Pitching and yawing on the sloped and uneven ground, they began driving fast across to where Purchand and Kamau were standing.

Kamau said even more urgently, 'I must go. I will tell the man to see you.'

'No...' started Purchand.

But Kamau was not listening as he began running down the lane. 'He will come to you. Tell him what you and I saw. Tell him, tell him.' Then Kamau was gone. Reflexively, Purchand stepped back into his yard and pulled his gate shut in haste, as the blue cars kept rushing to the lane.

He did not enter his house. His mind moved agitatedly over the words Kamau had been pressing upon him. 'Tell him, tell him.' Disturbed, he began to go over Kamau's urgent pleading, but this was cut short by the sounds of persons running outside, and then of shouts, 'Halt. *Simama.* Halt.' Gun shots followed loudly. Inside his yard, Purchand moved back to the gate and looked anxiously through a gap in the corrugated iron sheets. He saw Kamau running back down the lane and into the bar yard opposite; there were more shots, and he saw Kamau fall. Then uniformed figures filled the small gap.

He stepped back instantly and jammed the wooden beam across the gate. But he could not move away. He was shaking. He pressed his head against the metal sheets to keep looking. The lane had filled up with police cars and a large number of policemen. The latter gathered and stood around the dead body. Some had run into the bar. They came out pushing all the patrons into the yard. Several were arrested. The body was picked up and thrown into the back of one of the police vehicles. It drove away and one by one the others followed.

Purchand remained leaning against his gate in shock. A long while passed before he registered the gathering dark and went in quickly.

'What was that?' his wife rushed up to him. 'What was happening? What was happening?'

'Nothing.'

'I heard loud noises.'

'Nothing.' He continued roughly, 'Haven't I told you to keep the children in in the evenings?'

His voice turned into a shout, 'Stay in that room,' and the family fell silent.

The next day, Purchand waited in his shop for the tall man in the white suit. But no one came. In the evening at home, Purchand went and stood against the gate looking out. The bar was deserted.

The following morning, he went looking for the man from Nairobi, not knowing what he would do if he found him. Not knowing whether he had agreed or not with himself to do what Kamau had told him. But the man had gone. The other shopkeepers said the man had told them that they should tell Kamau if they knew anything. He had also left the name of a lawyer in Nairobi to whom people who wanted to help could go.

But now Kamau was dead.

Purchand was without an answer. Nor did he search for an answer or a direction. He could not agree to do what Kamau was asking of him. Yet he could not put away from his mind what Kamau had said. He wanted to do it. He could not possibly do it. He was angry with Kamau for having left him with the problem. He was angry with himself because he could not resolve it. His life in the small township had not prepared him to answer such a question. He had always thought he was not among those who should answer questions like these. These matters were not his business. And now Kamau was saying they were. Now he kept feeling that they were his business. His frightened mind threw up no answers.

He had never asked himself what he stood for. But in the family's rooms, the principal pictorial decorations, apart from the representations of gods and goddesses, were the images on large long-expired calendars. The leftover from the year 1947 showed Gandhi. The Mahatma, in his usual frugal dress and sandals, was striding into the future. Another similar leftover, of the year 1949, showed Gandhi and Nehru in the well-known reproduction of them seated on the Congress platform of earlier years, leaning towards each other in intimate conversation, master and pupil. It would have been difficult for Purchand to have explained what these retained calendar pictures, this homage, meant in terms of his personal choices. He could not have said why he had left them there year after year. But they had remained there as a conscious decision. And now was there a dissociation between whatever was on the wall and the life he was living below it?

He admitted to himself that he was not supposed to accept falsity such as Rebeka's in a court. Was the distance he had kept between those pictures on the wall and what he did lessening then?

Every evening he looked out at that main road from where those blue police station wagons had rushed towards them. He felt responsible. Then a few hours later in the light of day, he felt he had nothing to do with them. He would want to turn away, but he could not move. And so, evenings, Purchand stood at his back gate looking out where he had seen Kenyatta come out and leave long before the woman had gone into the bar with Kamau. Where Kamau had been killed.

Those evenings stretched into chronic incapacity. Days passed. Yet, when another *dukawalla* said he was driving to Nairobi the next day and there was a place in the car, Purchand quickly agreed to accompany him. He would go to the lawyer in Nairobi. There was no one here he could tell. That was why he had done nothing.

He felt better on the long drive to Nairobi. The following day, he dressed more formally and walked to the street where the lawyer's office was. He could not miss Government Road, everyone knew this main street. Then he walked up and down the shaded pavement outside the entrance of the building. And did it again. And again. Finally, he did not enter the offices and walked away. Too many days had passed, his story could not help anybody now, they would not need him or what he had seen any longer.

Two days later, he was back in Ol Kalou. When the following year, in April, the Magistrate at Kapenguria gave his judgment and said, *'P.W. 17, Rebeka, a witness of Christian conviction, gave her evidence in a forthright manner and clearly, and I accept her testimony that she saw the First Accused Kenyatta in the room behind the bar and heard him. No defence witness contradicted her…'*, Purchand never read it. He never read the newspapers.

He did not know what the court had said. He had by then left Ol Kalou. He had moved the family to Nairobi and never told anyone what he and Kamau had witnessed.

Fifteen years later, in 1968, Purchand again left. This time, it was the country.

He was one of the thousands who moved that year in what was locally called the 'exodus'. On his late-night arrival in the cold of the suburban airport of Stansted near London, their plane was met by a few journalists. They asked each passenger as they emerged, 'Did you have any difficulties?' In his answer, Purchand said, 'Yes. We are being thrown out. We left because the government does not want us. They do not want us to do business.'

Who was nearby to tell that waiting press, and Purchand himself, that no government had driven him out, that it was his own past, and the past of his own community, that had done this, that had brought him to this chill land?

During the preceding decades, like him, the community had fallen into keeping silent. It had thus stopped knowing, then stopped understanding, what was going on around it. Like him, it had not taken its witness to where it could have counted.

In those years, the community had emptied itself of its store of, and perception of, its own earlier rich part in the country's struggle. It had gradually let slip its place in the daily discourse in the colony over dignity and freedom. It had so distanced itself that it had become bankrupt of relevance, unable any longer to comprehend the sources of power in the country and their contesting directions. And by that, rendered itself unfit to make the final choices for itself and its members.

Thus, when the events of 1963 presented alternatives, the community, like Purchand, could not make a decision. The choice was simple to those who understood: to continue their life in Kenya as Kenyans as before, or to keep some other nationality and leave, and let Kenya get on with its destiny.

But by then, those who had not been following what had been going on around them had become ill equipped to make that decision. They had first looked for leaders to tell them what to do. But soon they had become distrustful of their own leaders, then of government statements, and finally of their own wavering judgments. Unable to unravel the logic of the laws pressing down on them, Purchand, and many who had become like him, finally imposed on the situation their own kind of logic: they decided that what they wanted was all the rights of one nationality, British, and also all the rights of another nationality, Kenyan. Because they said they were born here, they wanted the right to stay in Kenya as before, and also the right to stay in Britain. They also felt that it was up to themselves to decide how to exercise all these rights simultaneously, and not for various laws, or those lost thirty years, to decide where they should stay or how to live here and there, or there and here.

Those who had ceased to oppose colonialism had moved inexorably to its acceptance. And then in surprise they now found that the acceptance had not exempted them from being the further victims of this wild dog phenomenon they had tried to keep clear of.

Having thus lived for years impervious to reality, they landed at Stansted. When they were asked that question by the press, it was the first time they had asked themselves why events had brought them on these flights. Searching their meagre reservoir of awareness of what had happened in the past years, they found only this: 'We left because the government does not want us. They do not want us to do business.'

This collective failure was not the only load Purchand was carrying. Within that meagre and light suitcase he had brought as the unwanted expellee he saw himself to be, unseen, but all too clearly felt, was the weight of Kamau's few words of so long ago. With each passing year, unobeyed, they had gotten heavier and heavier. Till Purchand could no longer lift their weight, and staying near those words had become unbearable. Then he left, bringing both these loads, this personal and that collective, and landed, still not aware that they were the same load.

Active in the Furtherance

'WHAT ARE YOU DOING,' shouted his elder brother. It was not a question. It was an accusation. It spoke of the unreason of Gosar's actions. It reflected the incomprehension in the family.

'What are you doing.'

Gosar could say nothing. They were in his own *duka* in Mweiga, just outside Nyeri, and it was July 1953. This was Bhai, his eldest brother, practically his father now that the old man was doddering.

Bhai kicked the nearest sack. 'This will finish you. Maybe all of us. You do not think of us. Only of yourself. And of your nonsense talk. What is this "politics"? It has nothing to do with you. You leave it alone. Our work is to run our shop. Without problems, and without interfering with the government.

'I can't recognize you anymore. What has got into you? I don't see the person we knew anymore. You seem to be somebody else. We have all helped you to learn. We have paid fees for you to study more. More than any of us were allowed to. Do not think that you are the only one who wanted to study. I, Arun, Prakash all wanted to. But we had to help the family. We never completed school. And now after we have worked so much, and made it possible for you to finish school, see how you are repaying us.'

Gosar could only remain silent.

'When you wanted to open this shop, who helped you? Who gave you money to start here?' Indeed Bhai had, and Gosar had always happily acknowledged that.

'Why don't you listen?'

The long remonstrance poured on and on, scoring lines of pain on Gosar's downcast face.

'Do you know what this will do to Ba? She is not well at all. She keeps asking about you and I have to lie. Why is he not coming to Nairobi? She asks all the time. Is he in danger? I cannot tell her the nonsense that you are doing. You leave these people alone to do their mischief. Come home. This is not your work. This is not your fighting.'

At these final words, Gosar's determination to remain silent was finally overcome, and involuntarily he cried out, 'It is. The Governor is killing people wrongly. We see it. We are *here*. We have been here for many years now. We see bodies all the time. Sometimes on the roads, sometimes in the forest,' pointing to the thick wooded areas surrounding the small *duka*. 'Sometimes even in town. There are fires all the time. Everybody should fight. All of us here. You too.'

Bhai was startled. 'Me?' His voice rose. 'What has this got to do with me? Or with any of us for that matter? That is not why you are here. You have to stop this. Come away for a while to Nairobi. Let Babu come here for a while. So you can stay away from all this. And stop what you are doing. Chhotubhai came up to Nairobi specially to tell me.' Chhotubhai was married to one of the old man's sisters. 'All our *duka* people in this district are talking about it. They have all heard what you are doing. Stop it, stop it, Gosar.'

'Bhai, I can't. We cannot just watch and do nothing. People are being killed, they have nothing to eat, their goats, their sheep, their few cows are all confiscated, they are beaten when they ask why, houses and food are burnt down, their small land is being taken away, they are being fined all together even for things they have not themselves done. Chhotubhai knows all this. Is it wrong to give food to those who have nothing to eat? To help persons who are injured? Can we turn them away? Our *duka* people who are complaining to you are afraid. They know that what has to be done is right. But they are afraid to do it.'

'I don't understand this type of talk. I am telling the family that I have done all I can. You give me back my money. I do not want to lose my money because you want to do foolish things. We don't do foolish things. I am going. Do not expect us to help you when you are in jail. They will put you in jail. Do you not see that? They will beat you. They will kill you. I have said what I have come to say.' At the door, Bhai turned, 'You refuse to listen to sense. Do what you want.' And as he left, 'When things go wrong, when you need help, don't come to us.'

But Gosar did. Many months later. At a dark hour of a night, dirty and worn, Gosar reached Bhai's house in Nairobi. Bhai and Bhabhi embraced him and took him in. 'God's pity, we still have you,' Bhai began. 'Thank Him you have seen reason and returned.' Gosar held on tight to his elder brother, yet shook his head in weariness and from a pocket took out a much folded and unfolded paper. He held it up to Bhai. Gosar was fortunate it only said:

GOVERNMENT NOTICE No. 5681
The Emergency Regulations, 1952
Order under Section 4
WHEREAS it appears to me that a substantial number of inhabitants of Mweiga have recently been active in the furtherance of the objects of Mau Mau, by virtue of the powers conferred on me under section 4D(1)(i), I hereby make the following Order:

The shop set out in the Schedule hereto shall be closed and shall remain closed for a period of one year, with effect from the date of this Order.

Mweiga   G. H. B. BEYTS
15th March 1954   District Officer
                                    i/c Mweiga/Ngobit
SCHEDULE
Gosar Maya Shah . . . . Plot No. 3, Mweiga

Midnight Shunt

THE ENGINE SLOWLY clanged towards them. Its headlight, unnaturally bright in the cold wet mist, steadily bored into the darkness and at them. They crouched further down into the shadowed ditch beside the tracks. The engine halted noisily. The pointsman jumped off the steps at the front of the engine and ambled to the point. He tugged at the lever to change the direction of the rails. The point switched. Now pushing the wagons it had brought, the engine moved backwards, and the train swung away onto the adjacent lines, draining the light away from the area.

After a while, the engine returned, having dropped off the wagons, and the place lit up again. The points were switched back. As the pointsman remounted the steps, the engine blew a short whistle and then a long one. It signalled those on the original side that it was returning to collect additional wagons. It had been doing this for the past two hours and would continue for another two, till all the wagons had been appropriately marshalled into the correct rakes of the morning's trains.

From the ditch, the two watchers had been observing the pattern carefully. More carefully, they had been observing the behaviour of the soldier who stood sentry at the points. It was March 1954, and the Mau Mau Emergency was in full spate. The freedom fighters in the forests needed weapons, and more importantly, needed ammunition with which to make effective the guns they already had. The two watchers worked together, more often than he did with her other roommates in River Road. They were close too. Sometimes she worked alone near the barracks where the English soldiers were at Kabete. Sometimes she was the courier to and from Defence Headquarters. He moved openly during the daytime, untrammelled, by reason of being Indian, by the need for passes and *kipande* identity documents. But at night he was busy, meeting messengers from the Aberdares, escorting collected weaponry deep into the supply chain to the forests, and then even later into the earliest hours, preparing memoranda of atrocities to send to London and the foreign press. Then back in an hour or two to his daytime job in the same colonial government's Statistics Department in the Treasury.

As the engine returned with the fresh wagons, the points shone again and the soldier was sharply lit up, his rifle a prominent outline. Each time, he would approach closer. The points would be changed. And the engine and wagons would move away. On the engine's way back, it would halt again while the points changed back. The short and long whistles would sound, and its departure would mark the return of darkness at the points. As the engine moved away, the soldier would first turn into a silhouette and then a camouflaged piece of the night. After the second hour, he had begun to sit on the high ballast of the adjoining tracks closer to the hedge.

In the third hour, when the watchers judged that his watchfulness was tiring with the repetitive and monotonous process and saw that he no longer patrolled around, the woman stood up.

After the engine had come back, the points had been changed, and it had moved away to deliver the fresh set of wagons, she walked carefully along the hedge towards the soldier. Nearer, she coughed gently.

'Who's there?' he called out, startled, quickly raising his rifle.

She stepped out slowly to become visible.

'Who are you? What do you want here?'

'It depends on what you want,' she said persuasively. 'How much money have you got?'

'Go away, go away,' he said in a frightened voice.

In response she began unbuttoning her blouse, then took it off, revealing her bare top.

The young man stared.

She said 'Do you have a shilling? Only a shilling. I need food.'

And stepped out of her skirt, revealing her unclothed figure.

Still staring at her, despite himself, he heard his own hoarse croak, 'Only fifty cents.'

She held out her hand. 'Hurry up before that thing comes back.'

She lay down invitingly on the grass verge next to the thick hedge. His hands moved between his pockets and his belt. Finally, holding on to his rifle, dropping his trousers, he tripped over her legs onto her. As he fumbled, the locomotive returned. She whispered, 'Shh,' pulling him deeper into the shadows and motionless. As he lay upon her, the engine's first short whistle sounded loudly. A figure stirred behind them. Out of the hedge, an arm emerged. Metal pushed against the man's side. His startled cry, the engine's second long whistle, and the shot were a single sound. The engine's clangour faded away. The place returned to stillness and deep darkness.

She pushed the inert body off with difficulty, and pulled herself up shakily. With trembling hands and distaste, she wiped the copious blood off herself. They moved in careful silence. Emptying the soldier's pockets, the man rolled the body into the kai apple hedge and pushed it in as deep as he could. While she dressed, he rifled through the soldier's ammunition pouch. There were two bullets. He showed them to her. It was a good night's work. Bullets were precious booty, collected in lots or singly, by any means possible, whether by last year's attack on Naivasha Police Station or by tonight's work. But bullets were an especially dangerous commodity to be found with. Before the declaration of the Emergency, only two criminal offences were punishable by a death sentence. As the Emergency deepened, the government changed the law to make another six offences punishable by death, making a total of eight capital offences, a statutory position unequalled anywhere else in the Empire. One of these was the unlawful possession of bullets. It was the provision most amenable to misuse by the police and bounty hunters, who regularly planted them on those they arrested.

Lifting the bullets with his handkerchief, he quickly pocketed them. Unsteadily, she joined him as he stood silently with the soldier's rifle, practiced in its handling. He would dispose of it through well-established channels to reach those who needed it most in the forests.

They waited motionless for a long while, listening for any sound of danger. Then, with the greatest caution, the two worked their way back and out of the railway yard. He had been holding her hand as they had retreated. But on the last corner, he drew her close to him, his hands moving.

'Not tonight, Guru darling,' she said tiredly, and gently disengaged to go. Then turned back, kissed him hard on the mouth, and melted away into the heavy dark of the landhies.

AFTERWORD

The statements attributed to the government and leaders in 'Learning' are factual and are drawn from official records and their own memoirs. The lines on bureaucracy in 'Room No. 8, Law Courts' are Stefan Zweig's, from his *The Post Office Girl* (London, Atrium Books / Zurich, Williams Verlag AG, 1982, translation by Joel Rotenberg).

P.N.

ACKNOWLEDGEMENTS

Villoo, my best editor, has remained a major part
in fashioning these stories. Eric Ng'maryo, a writer
himself, had, as in my earlier collection, edited drafts of
several of these stories. To both, thanks and love. Many
thanks too to Judy Gathungu for support over the long
period of preparation.

Hedda and Hermann Steyn had again given the
shelter of uninterrupted silence to bring these stories
to completion, together with accompanying music to
keep remembering. More thanks and love.

I again thank Mzee Balubhai Sarvaiya for the many
discussions on the years these stories cover.

The story 'Initiation' first appeared in slightly different
form in the magazine *Parsiana* (Mumbai), which I
gratefully acknowledge.

Ciira Hirst and Edward Miller fortunately agree with
the wisdom of Ecclesiastes that of making many books
there is no end, but fortunately also believe that the
consequent weariness of the flesh is however no bar.
To them, my ongoing admiration and gratitude. Again.

P.N.